MINK

BY

Robyn Rolison-Hanna

Cover Artwork and Interior
Illustrations By
Olga Dunayeva

ARCTIC WOLF PUBLISHING

This book is dedicated to my mother, *Norma Rolison,* who gave me the gift of reading, and an unwavering love of books. This book would not have been possible without her.

Arctic Wolf Publishing
http://www.arcticwolfpublishing.com
ISBN - 10: 0-9817472-3-X
ISBN - 13: 978-0-9817472-3-1

Printed in the United States of America

Table of Contents:

Prologue

Apennine Mountains

The hills roll behind Vatican City; the dome of Basilica of Saint Peter, can be seen in the distance peaking above the forest's tree line, only to become a speck, reaching toward a brilliant blue sky, so clear one can almost see God.

The forest beyond yawns and stretches in all different directions, enjoying its solitude. The quiet morning now awake, yet still sleepy, is drenched with the sweet aroma of the vineyards that lay beyond.

Deep plump purple grapes, covered in morning dew, spread over the land like a solid blanket of green vines. Olive groves provide shade and a sweet haven from the sun for lizards and toads. Butterflies flutter and bees hum from one flower to the next.

Squirrels, most playful this time of day, race and jut in and out of their moss and wood covered homes. Orchid patches carpet the hillside under a canopy of beech and fir trees. Even shy Marsican brown bears come out to wrestle and play.

…The day is anew.

Deeper into the forest. Nature, now fully awake, shies away from the depth in this part of the forest. The woodlands grow even darker. Sunlight cannot penetrate this bleakness. Whispering pine shrubs with their long stiff needles stand erect like sentinels waiting for something to happen by. The velvety grassland halts, as though an invisible barrier prevents its continuance.

Darker yet, is the dirt and gravel road that leads to a place where no living thing will go, willingly. Jogging armies of insects turn back as they approach this road with a sign stabbed into the ground that reads **NO TRESPASSING**, over a picture of a skull and crossbones. The road has one way in and one way out... but once in, no one ever comes out.

So many eyes in the dark... eyes that change from one moment to the next. Closed eyes that can't see anymore. Frightened eyes that don't scream anymore. Half-closed eyes that don't care anymore. Angry eyes that can't fight anymore.

In their enclosures, they wait quietly. Parents clutch their children. Males clutch their females. Some have no one left to clutch, so they clutch the wire mesh that imprisons them. They know where they are. They know what happens here.

"It wouldn't be so bad if he gave us a bullet in the head," someone whispered.

"Shut up," another one answered.

"I can handle a bullet," he replied, apparently talking to no one. ...This one had lost his mind.

"I said, shut-up... no one wants to hear this...." the one next to him said again.

"I just don't think I can handle an injection of insecticide. Did you ever see anyone die shot up with insecticide, and sometimes when they gas, they don't even wait until we are dead before they start to skin us."

"I told you I didn't want to hear this. You're loco!"

"I hope you're right. Maybe I am mad and I'll wake up in my own bed and laugh later because this was only a mad mink's foray into a nightmare. A pretty *real* nightmare."

"Just keep your thoughts to yourself. No one wants to hear them."

"Sometimes they electrocute. But that's not a sure-fire death either. They stick this thin rod...."

The one next to him hissed and grabbed at his neck. "If you don't shut up, I'll finish you off here and now."

"Please. I could only pray for that. Pray for a bullet or a twisted neck. Snap and it's over...."

"No... it's not over..." the one next to him dropped his fore arms. "... It will never be over...."

...Guisseppi Tucci stood in front of a massive cabinet in the repository, looking at long shelves of insecticides. His eyes wandered to the next shelf down, the shelf that held all his different size and models of electric mink prods. The bottom shelf held large canisters of carbon monoxide and carbon dioxide gases.

While harvesting and trapping minks he very seldom employed methods recommended by the Italian Veterinary Association to ensure the animal a quick and painless death. Who cares? They were animals for God's sake. What was the world coming to? He stood and tapped his index finger against his cheek trying to decide what he was in the mood for this morning. Um… he closed his eyes and pointed.

"*Eny Meeny Miny Moe…. Catch a minky by the toe… If it hollers can't let it go… Eny Meny Miny Moe….*" Tucci opened his eyes and smiled.

He reached up and began grabbing bottles and syringes and placing them into boxes. Insecticides. He smiled again… his favorite. They kind of did a little tap dance after getting a shot of this. He was glad his finger hadn't pointed to the gas tanks. He felt like a willing participant this morning, and the gas he attached to the engine of his tractor and channeled in their enclosures, took all the fun out of actually participating, since he was one side, and they were on the other.

He heard that their eyes and lungs burned and that it was a painful death, but in a pinch, nothing was faster. If it were up to him, he'd just *whack* off their heads. *But can't hurt that fur now can we?* He closed the boxes and placed them in the back of his tractor. He lumbered into the driver's seat and started the engine.

He planned to sell the organic manure to some farmers for their fields and vineyards, and all the protein-rich carcasses for compost or feed. He made sure he put everything to good use. *Here we go little buddies… Let's make it a good one…."*

* * * *

Chapter One

Castle de Ulderico

Present Day Rome

Z eto came from a long line of Roman counts and countesses. Although he was prone to bragging, but truths be known, he considered his blood bluer than most European kings and queens. He is a descendant of the Ulderico family, one that could trace their origins all the way back to the first mink that originally came from North America.

He is Count Zeto Pantaleone Ulderico. Often you could find him at *Castello Di Ulderico*, his palace den, surrounded by an army of guards and servants, a handful of friends, showing off portraits of family members that had in one way or another become ornaments around famous humans' necks....

"Oh and here is Uncle Salvatore and Aunt Rita," he said as he turned the page of a very large family album he displayed on his coffee table.

He elbowed his best friend and sidekick, Muccino Alberdini, who had heard about and seen each and every one of these creepy looking pictures a hundred times before, but he didn't like being impolite, so he sat and listened and nodded and pinched himself repeatedly so that he wouldn't fall asleep.

Muccino's motto was.... "Never bite the hand that feeds you or lends you money."

"That is my poor Uncle Salvatore with the longer snout. I

1

am told that I resemble him. I don't see it, but that's what I'm told. And Aunt Rita is behind him and that's actually Queen Victoria's neck and shoulder's that mink stole is wrapped around. Actually Uncle Salvatore was Viscount Salvatore until he married that commoner and was disowned by his entire family. Now look at him! This is what happens when there are no guards protecting you... that's what my father, God rest his soul, always said."

Muccino nodded. He was getting hungry again. He wondered if Zeto had any of that delicious muskrat pie left over that cook had made this morning?

Muccino or Mooch got his nickname from what he did best. Mooch was a world-class sponger. He took what he could get and from Zeto he got plenty. It wasn't that he was cheap by any means. He liked to think of himself as a rather prudent chap. He didn't have the title of *Count* nor a Count's deep pockets to dig into.

...He patted his belly. He wondered if he was putting on more weight.

Zeto turned toward his pudgy friend and removed his reading glasses. "Did I tell you that our lineage has been linked with King Orsino?" Mooch always rubbed his belly right below his white spot when he was hungry. His dusky chestnut tail arched back behind him. "Mooch you could not possibly be hungry again. You just ate not an hour ago!"

"I can't help it," he whined. "I have a fast metabolism."

2

"You'd never know it by looking at you," Zeto added sarcastically as he closed his favorite book. "What is it that you want cook to fix for you now?"

"I thought if there was any of that muskrat pie left, just a small sliver mind you," Mooch said holding up his index finger and thumb to show how small a portion he wanted. He rubbed his paws together. "Some of the roasted magpie goose would be nice with maybe a slice of vole and for that I will be forever indebted."

"You already are forever in my debt." Zeto stood motioning for a footmink. "Please tell cook that Mr. Muccino would like the roasted goose, a slice of vole and muskrat pie for dessert. Tell him to serve it in the formal dining room. That will be all. Oh wait... and a bottle of our best. Cook will know what I want."

Count Zeto Pantaleone Ulderico had always been considered extremely handsome with his dark almost black pelt, a muscular frame and a slightly longer than the average adult male mink length of 15 centimeters. His tail far exceeded 20 centimeters and most female minks found him hard to resist. His dark fur was of the highest quality due primarily, if you asked him, from a long line of superior ancestors consisting mostly of princes, dukes, counts, viscounts, a few barons, and one king. *How could he not have turned out this way...*he would ask himself? Ancestrally speaking, he was in every way the perfect mink and he knew it. The only flaw, if it was to be considered a flaw at all, was the reading glasses that he had to wear.

His eyes were well adapted to day vision, but he was not nocturnal, in fact it was sometimes difficult for him to see anything at night since he never had to depend upon his eyesight for night hunting being that he had never hunted a day in his life.

Just the thought of flattening his body along grubby lakes and stream beds gave him tremors and then sliding quietly around on his stomach in smelly dirt and then pouncing on some unaware prey caused beads of perspiration to dampen his brow. No, hunting was not for him. His father once wanted to teach him the mechanics of the hunt, just for sport, which sent his mother, the Contessa of Ulderico, into the vapors. His mother, Arabella to close friends, Bella to his father, fussed so much about the Great Barn Owl, golden eagles, the lynx and foxes that she sometimes took to her bed.

Zeto made a point of not venturing out into the night often. He was well aware that palace guards protected him whatever the situation called, however, he felt better not having to put anyone in danger, *especially not himself* and because of this, he met female minks only at various soirees such as balls and dinner parties, hosted usually by his mother. It wasn't that he lacked female attention; on the contrary, many beautiful debutantes and mate seekers flocked to his side when he was forced to attend those dreadful affairs which seemed to peak between February and April, however, they all seemed to just bore him to death.

Most females found the Count moody and sullen, usually

standing off by himself in some corner of the room in a perpetual frown. This didn't; however, seem to hinder them from batting their eyes and doing a lot of high pitched cackling whenever they got the chance, which never failed to grate on his nerves.

He often wondered at the night's end, if there had ever been any real conversation or talk of any value with the entire lot of them? Could any of the females he met formulate a single original thought or opinion he sometimes wondered?

Why did any of it matter? Zeto liked his life the way it was. A bachelor he was and a bachelor he would remain. He enjoyed his books; an education had been very important to his family, but sometimes he questioned what it was all for? It wasn't as if he could really use it for anything purposeful. It was unthinkable that he should actually *work* like a common laborer, so what was the point he sometime pondered of so much education to use absolutely nowhere except in shallow conversation?

He sat back in his chair watching Mooch stuff his face. He sometimes contemplated if there was a finite end to his stomach. Did he eat because he felt hunger or did he eat out of habit?

He lifted a glass of vino to his lips. *Brunello di Montalcino*, yes, a glass of Brunello was just what the doctor ordered. Brunello was a favorite, which he kept well stocked in his wine cellars with many other vintages. He sat across from Mooch sipping his wine while watching him shovel large fork fulls of roasted fowl into his mouth. He longed to enjoy something that much.

"Mooch," he began, placing his wine glass down, "What is it about food that you enjoy so much? I mean food is food. It nourishes the body, keeps it moving and is vital to continue our species or any species for that matter, but you eat with so much panache, that I was sitting here watching you and wondering what it is about food that causes so much enjoyment for you? I don't think I ever enjoyed anything in my life as much as it appears you enjoy eating."

Mooch started to speak as he always did while still chewing, and oftentimes spewed particles of food spritzed the air in front of him, giving whoever was in his line of fire a good food shower. This never failed in making Zeto cringe, but he put up with a lot of Mooch's table faux pas and general bad manners because he was a distant cousin and a poor one at that.

"I love food!" Mooch said with his mouth still full. "And it tastes *especially* delicious when it is hunted for you and prepared for you, and the only job that I am required to do is to eat it. How could I *not* enjoy it? Your problem is that everything is handed to you so you can't enjoy anything because you don't know what it is like to actually *work* for something."

"That's ridiculous!" Zeto picked up his wine glass and killed what was left. Had he actually finished the entire bottle himself minus the one that Mooch was now sipping? Looking closer at the bottle, he could see that it was empty. He was not use to indulging in spirits.

"…I'll have you know that I have accomplished and achieved much in my life through hard work and perseverance. Not everything has been handed to me!"

"Yeah right!" Mooch chuckled as he pointed his fork at him. "Give me an example?"

"Oh, for Goodness sake, I am not going to sit here and rattle off a list of my hard earned accomplishments just to appease you. We could be here all night!"

"No," Mooch said putting down his fork. He crossed his fore arms in front of himself and leaned back in his chair. "All I want is one. No list, because we both know you couldn't come up with one. I just want to hear you tell me about *uno*."

Zeto was calmly aware of the ready challenge in Mooch's eyes. Even if he had procured a little too much wine, surely he could cough up one. He pulled himself ramrod straight, leaned over the table and glared down at Mooch.

"I have obtained several post graduate degrees in Mink Sociology and a secondary degree in Mink Evolution and have also studied under the famous sociologist, Enrico Constantini, not to mention Savino Toscana, known world wide for his writing and lectures on European Mink Evolution and why it is now approaching the "threatened species" status. I have not been idle." Did he just slur the word *idle*? "And I don't know what all your pointless rambling is about. I have done my share of hard work and I refuse to sit here and defend myself especially to you, especially about *hard work*."

Mooch squinted his beady little eyes, scrutinizing Zeto and then he pushed his almost empty plate of food away from him and rested his head in his paws.

"Have you ever been to the wetlands my friend? Are you a molter? I know you have *never* hunted, but have you ever swum underwater or for that matter, have you been near a body of water period? Have you ever mated?"

"Now you're getting personal...." Zeto started to rise from the table, but thought better of it when a sudden surge of blood rushed to his head making him dizzy.

"Hold on." Mooch stood from his chair and strutted around the table as though he was the King Mink. "I have the water habits of an otter because I am forced to. I can, and have escaped from most predators. My back webbed legs are used for the purpose in which God intended. I can dive from 6 meters high into a body of water and I can swim to a depth of more than 30 meters. I know my body doesn't look particularly in the peak of shape at the moment, but I have worked hard to master all these skills."

He paused for a moment. "You live in this palace paradise on over three square kilometers of open territory, but have you ever walked along its wooded streams?

Did you ever discover that you have marshes on your land or that there are several other inhabitants living on your precious grounds with you? ...I have.

You have woodchuck holes everywhere, minks that have

8

burrows amongst your rocks cavities and hollow trees. Have you ever met any of them? I am sure you haven't because they constitute the way the other half live, and Lord only knows that you *never* rub elbows with the other half.... "

"I rub elbows with you don't I?" Zeto said, ramming the point home. "And, correct me if I am wrong, but I have known you all my life Mooch and I have never heard, let alone seen any of these remarkable feats you now tell me that you possess?"

"Because I am humble, and have never been prone to boasting or showing off."

"That's debatable." Zeto said with a shrug.

Mooch smiled down at him, and then his expression became serious again. "Do you know what an insect taste like?"

"And your point ...*being?*" Zeto asked slowly pulling on one of his whiskers, a gesture he had done since youth when encountering frustration or when deeply engrossed in thought.

"My point being that as your best friend, *and only friend,* you need to grow Zeto. You need to venture out and see what's here in this world and grow my friend. Grow!"

"So, in other words I can feel like I have really grown as a mink if I eat an insect?" Zeto felt a slight churning in his stomach at the mere thought and wished he had eaten something, but God forbid never an insect.

"You live like a monk-mink in a monastery instead of enjoying your life," said Mooch.

He swung his arms out over the room and added, "You

have all this and for what? To sit in attendance at those stiff parties your mother and relatives throw or reading books and listening to opera?

If I had all that you were born into, I would at least be enjoying something, somewhere with someone. Lunches, business meetings, elaborate speeches at charity functions, and to your credit, you do a wonderful job, and though I am not trying to take anything away from that, I have to ask… are you living your life?

I know that because of your position, being a Count and all, that many of those things are compulsory, but do you ever think that you are going to die before having lived? Don't you think life needs some balance?

When was the last time you can say that you were having so much fun that time disappeared and you never knew where it went? It has to be the best feeling in the world. Did that ever happen to you?

If so, I have never heard of it, or seen it. So for once in your life Zeto, do something; please just do something for fun!

We need to get out of here for a change, you and me, and go somewhere and have an adventure, the kind where we lose all track of time. How could you not be going stir nutty crazy sitting around here doing the same blah things night in and night out?

Blah… blah… and more blah. Bor-ing!"

"You never seem to be too *blahed* eating me out of house and home," Zeto said. He picked up a knife and sliced himself a small sliver of muskrat pie. He needed to put something into his now empty stomach. But even the thought of muskrat pie seemed to turn his stomach.

Mooch walked back to his chair and popped the last morsel of piecrust into his mouth. "I'm taking off." He adjusted the collar of his jacket. "Life is in motion Zeto and tonight I plan to be in motion with it."

He moved in front of a mirror, some ornate sixteenth century royal heirloom hanging above a high-legged server, and reached into his jacket pocket to produce a comb to brush his now bent and droopy red whiskers. For a moment he wondered why they went limp on him after eating. He hated when that happened.

"We're young Zeto. We're handsome. You and me, we got it going, so let's go do something. Let's shake it up a little bit couz! Come with me tonight and let's live a little or would you rather stay home and look at more pictures of dead relatives?"

Had Zeto been of his right mind he would have refused without so much as a bat of his eye, but tonight he wasn't in his particular right mind. He had far too much wine and he was feeling bolder, and even if Mooch was nothing more than a puffed up bag of wind, he had thrown down the gauntlet and these unfair allegations launched at him tonight could not be ignored. What was he... a mink or a mouse?

"Alright Mooch." He surprised himself at how calm those

words were spoken. "I will go with you tonight not because you have tried to shame my mink being by your talk of all the physical feats involved in our natural habitat that I obviously lack. No. Trying to goad and humiliate me hasn't worked cousin. I am going with you tonight because I am naturally curious about how the other side live. I have studied the mink society for many years and now I want to see what you think I have apparently been missing."

Zeto took his reading spectacles from inside his vest pocket and placed them on the table. "As you are well aware, I see nothing in the dark, so I insist we take a few guards along with us for protection."

Mooch belched loudly, patted his belly and said, "No can do my friend. Just you and me Pal. No security. We are living free and dangerous. We're on our own tonight."

Frequently Zeto wondered why he tolerated Mooch and his deplorable manners for all these years. The judgmental side, and pretty much the only side of his personality believed that his sometime crass cousin derived much pleasure and attention from belching open mouthed, and expelling gas in mixed company, not to mention the snorting sounds he made when laughing and of course his revolting habit of talking with his mouth full. When they were teenminkers, these things were funny, he even remembers a laugh or two at some of Mooch's antics, but now they were adult male minks and it wasn't so funny anymore.

He didn't seem to care at all about offending anyone's

sensibilities. It was as if those around him were either invisible or didn't matter. Mooch was a mink without inhibitions--none whatsoever. It was bad enough that he alienated colleagues and annoyed male friends, or that he repelled female minks as well, which did nothing to elevate his status, but the worst part of it was that none of it ever seemed to bother him.

To Mooch, it was a laughing matter. Everything was a laughing matter. It was all a big joke to him. He believed life was too short to be taken seriously. And as much as he hated to admit it, sometimes Zeto wished he could be a little more like that--not to care so much about what other minks thought, not to live in a high-profile fish bowl surrounded by peering eyes.

He would never employ Mooch's atrocious manners, but to be a little freer in thought and deed, to shed so many stringent rules and responsibilities. He had never known that kind of freedom.

On the other hand, Mooch was not without his merits. During those rare moments without buffoonery, he could be quite endearing and entertaining. He was an intelligent conversationalists and a wicked iconoclast. Zeto could even venture to say that he could be down right charming at times. Mooch had stepped into this present day *stooge*, a part he had adopted many years ago while they were away at school together and so far remained that forever juvenile.

Zeto came to the conclusion that it was all contrived, so that Mooch could do all the *rejecting* but never be the one *rejected*.

For as long as Zeto could remember Mooch battled the bulge. He bore perpetual *chunker* taunts starting with his father at birth. He claimed he had been born overweight, not the normal pea pod size; but more like an over-ripe plump red tomato and like him, he had also been born without siblings.

His one passion in life was food and he savored each meal and in-between meals and the in-between-in-between meals. Actually Mooch lived pretty much to eat, constantly drawing attention to his overt robustness, by patting his belly, making funny remarks about his winter, spring, summer and fall blubber, and that dear ol' dad had waited for him to *pop* before he took off.

Yet, Zeto also detected serious undertones to many of Mooch's seemly flippant remarks about his appearance, serious underlying comments about the crummy physical make-up that he had been handed. Mooch had amicably tolerated many stings like an entertaining clown, but nowadays he made sure that he jabbed first and the hardest at himself before anyone else got a crack at it.

On rare occasions, he would make subtle remarks about his pelt or his lack thereof. He was self-conscious about it, always comparing it with other male minks they both knew socially. He especially compared his pelt to Zeto's, since his pelt was considered exceptional because of its denseness and rich dark black coffee hue.

He remembered that Mooch once told him that one could always change their weight but nothing could be done about a mink's pelt situation. It was all in the DNA. His coat was not considered fashionable nor desirous because it was basically thin

14

and a mousy sort of indeterminate reddish-brown and he knew the ladies *always* went for the minks that had the thickest pelts in razzle-dazzle dark colors.

No amount of molting or lengthy spells spent outdoors during the heart of even the most sever winters had altered it. In the spring it was even worse.

Zeto often thought on the matter of pelts and could never understand why pelts were so important to the opposite sex. His eyes as well... what was it about his eyes that females went on and on about? Did they not all have the same basic brown eyes? Apparently to the....

"HEY... ZEE-TOOO!" Mooch snapped his claws in front of his face. "Hello... hey... where are you? Are we going to sit here all night or are we going?"

Zeto wiped his paws over his face and took a deep breath. "Just give me a minute."

"No, because if I give you a minute your OCDness will kick in and you will talk your self out of our night adventure. We are going. Get up and let's go."

"Well at least give me a second to inform everyone that we are headed out for the evening and I need to grab a pair of stronger glasses."

"No one needs to know where we are going or what we are doing. You're a grown mink for heaven's sake.... Leave everything up to me. I know exactly where to take you. And you won't need reading glasses for where we're going. My eyes are sharp enough

15

for both of us tonight, so let's *GOOOOOOOOO*."

"I hope you know what you're doing," Zeto said as he rose and began to follow Mooch to the entrance hall.

…Mooch was reeling that Zeto had actually accepted his challenge and was stepping his royal majesty's big toe-claw outside the walls of his self-imposed comfort zone without his ever present *goons*. This was *not* like Zeto. Yes, Zeto was a diplomat. He could placate and talk circles around any argument and was a top negotiator, yet he chose to allow Mooch to win this one. Mooch scratched his ear. When he thought he had him finally figured him out **...BAM...** he did something to offset it. Zeto was a good mink, there was no finer one made, but if you wanted to hang around for the long haul, you had to continually appeal to his vanity. Yet tonight, he did just the opposite, and was getting his way. He shook his head. He would never figure him out.

Personally, Zeto would feel more secure if he knew his palace security were a comfortable distance away, watching. His bodyguards came from long lines and generations of palace security and were considered to be one of the most ferocious groups of ex-soldier minks to be reckoned with. They were considered vicious by all, but also loyal to a fault, and he would make sure the ones posted outside would *not* follow. He supposed he had to prove his maleness to someone and he was not quite sure if it was to Mooch or to himself.

****

Chapter Two

Crabby's

"How much longer are we going to be out here?" Zeto asked impatiently. "Mooch! Would you please stop for a breath! Holding on to your back appendage and traveling at this speed is not exactly my idea of a good time. Jeeeez!" Zeto gave Mooch's tail a hard tug. "For the love of God, would you …STOP!"

"Hold on!" Mooch yelled, half turning. "Hey! Stop that, you're ruining my concentration."

Zeto gave his tail another hard jerk....

"I said… stop yanking on me like that. The tail's not made of plastic!"

"I asked you how much longer?" Zeto picked up a faint odor of something wild in the air, and off to his right in the distance, he was sure he heard what sounded like a snapping twig and crisp patches of leaves crunching underfoot, or was it them?

"Be patient, cousin. I know that patience is not one of your virtues, but you're just going to have to wait a few more minutes and I promise you that I'll have you eating the best mouth-watering crab cakes you have ever tasted in your life. It is right over the ridge. Just hang in there, or should I say *on* there. We will be there in a couple minutes."

"How did I know you would be taking me to a place that serves food!" Zeto sniffed again, opened his nostrils as wide as they would go. *Nothing.* *Surely Mooch with his keen olfactory senses and outstanding auditory abilities would have picked something up if they were in some kind of trouble.* "Forever thinking about your stomach."

"Hey listen, I'm on a mission to show you a good time tonight and my stomach has nothing to do with it." Mooch chuckled. "Seeing is believing, and shortly you will be *seeing*... and thanking me for it later."

Swallowed in darkness, and despite his calm demeanor, Zeto was becoming more rattled by the minute as he trailed behind Mooch holding onto his tail for dear life. Clutching Mooch's tail and moving as quickly as they were going had to be one of the strangest sensations Zeto had ever felt. It was like being blind and running at full speed in an unfamiliar open space knowing that at any moment you were going to plow straight ahead, head first into something hard, like a jutting tree trunk or bolder, but at the same time, trying hard not to lose footing and topple over. What had he been thinking when he agreed to do this? That was the problem. He hadn't been thinking....

He knew if he asked Mooch to turn around and take him back home, that there would be a lot of grumbling and complaining, but Zeto knew Mooch would reluctantly comply. The thought truly crossed his mind more than once. This tiny voice in his head kept repeating a never-ending litany of all the reasons why this little rendezvous was not such a great idea after all and why it would be best to just turn around go back home.

First and more importantly, he could see nothing. He was as good as a blind bat without echolocation. His crippled eyesight was so poor under this moonless black sky that he kept thinking that if something should happen to Mooch, he would never be able to find his way back home which caused a shiver of panic to ripple through him at the thought of being so dependent and helpless and he did not like either of those two feelings, and couldn't remember the last time he had felt them.

He could feel himself break out into a fit of nerves at his own uselessness. He believed his sense of smell had also atrophied along with his night vision, so smelling his way back would be also out of the question. And then there was his hearing, which he didn't have to be told was not up to snuff. He had no business being out here in this wilderness, at night without them.

The one thing that did surprise him was that a mink as marginally overweight as Mooch could move this fast? How long had he been sprinting and how long had he been hanging on?

"…We are almost to "Crabby's." Mooch announced as if he knew what was on Zeto's mind and turning his head ever so slightly, added, "You'll thank me for this when it's all over."

Zeto stretched his neck to one side and could see what appeared to be a lighted area up ahead.

"Now that's original. Crabby's… crab cakes."

"It's not called Crabby's because of the crab cakes."

Mooch snickered.

"It is called Crabby's because the owner and cook, Benoit Barouche', is an unrelenting crab, pinchers and all. You wait till you meet him and you'll understand. That mink can be meaner than a snake, but he makes the best dang crab dishes this side of the Tiber.

If you can get past his rather unpleasant disposition, you'll never eat better tasting crab cakes in your entire life. I believe there was some kind of scandal a long time ago in some small place in North America called New Orleans. I don't know all the details, but rumor has it that he's cranky and nasty, sometimes downright rabid because he had some sort of *situation* over there.

Through various grapevines I heard that he was involved in a love affair gone bad. No one knows for sure, I certainly don't, and frankly I really don't care. No one would dare ask him, but there is much speculation floating around about it.

I heard this New Orleans place where he lived, is heavily populated with French Caribbean minks and many of the dishes that have become so popular here were concocted over there.

He has a lot of spicy crayfish and jambalaya dishes that he apparently took from there. Minks from everywhere flock here for his callaloo too. I'm surprised you never heard of this place. Who knows his real story?"

Mooch looked over at Zeto and shrugged. "And there are several different ones."

Zeto rolled his eyes. "And I am dying to hear them all…

my life will never be the same until I do."

"Listen bud, new latitudes, new attitudes! And you're going to learn absolutely nothing with that attitude! The people in there may not travel in our same social circles, but the food Crabby prepares is fit for any king"

Mooch stopped in front of what appeared to be a cozy little abandoned muskrat den. It looked from what Zeto could make out to be a rather large establishment, some type of old hollowed out tree stump with an open door. Loud music drifted from its small entrance. Sounded like Jazz with some intermixture of Blues, he could hear a saxophone singing a sad tune. Zeto let go of Mooch's tail and tried to dust himself off.

"And Zeto... um... try as much as you can to *ditch* the aristocratic hooey and blend. We's mixin' with the normal folks, you know... that other half."

"What do you mean "the aristocratic *hooey?*" Zeto frowned indignantly. "I am an aristocrat! How else am I supposed to act?" Zeto could not believe this mink's audacity. His head suddenly felt very heavy, as though he was carrying a bowling ball around inside his skull.

"Don't take it personal. I just mean that no one needs to know that you are the Count of Ulderico and all that. That might put them off. Be somebody else tonight, just a regular *Pisano'.*"

"What I am is insane... insane for listening to you in the first place. Regular guy... what does that mean? How does one act like a regular guy?"

"Just act like me. I've been known to act like one on occasion."

"You're serious aren't you?" Zeto snapped, shaking his head *"NO"*. "Let me make something absolutely clear Mr. Muccino.... so listen carefully. If you think for a second, that I am going to walk around inside that dump, belching, snorting, breaking wind, and slopping food into my mouth, you've got another thing coming to you."

Zeto walked behind Mooch as they neared the entrance of Crabby's. "You have nerve. I cannot pretend to be anyone other than who I am and if *that other half* doesn't care for it, then that's just too bad... What the heck am I?"

Zeto stopped suddenly and sniffed the air. "That smell? Jeez cousin! Is that you again?"

"No, it is not me again; I beg your pardon.... Now you really *are* starting to insult me. This ain't no Taj Mahal. This is what Crabby's smells like. Like I said, he cooks strictly seafood and Creole dishes, and like most *normal* minks, present company excluded, he oftentimes overstocks large quantities of food. Now if a few crab or crayfish or some mice sausage turn bad now and again, well, what the hey."

He stopped and turned around. "Now look Zeto, will you please try to relax? You're as stiff as a beaver tail. Can't you take it down a couple notches and relax? This isn't going to be enjoyable if you continue your bellyaching. Let yourself have a little fun here?

24

You're worse than a dang shrewmouse." He reached for the door and pulled it open.

Zeto turned and looked through the door and then he looked back at Mooch. "You made me this way with that moronic comment about concealing my identity and for the love of God, how can I ingest anything in there when the mere smell of the place is enough to make me heave?"

Mooch grabbed Zeto's fore arm and shoved him through the opening. "After a few minutes in there, you'll hardly notice it-- nobody does."

Zeto looked around and was relieved that candlelight lit the entire room well enough for him to see. He fished around in his coat pocket until he found one of his hallmarked handkerchiefs, monogrammed with the family crest that he never left home without, and discretely held it up to his nose to block reeking dead carcass smells. Mooch stepped to his side, and together they headed toward a corner booth along the far back wall and sat down.

"Hey Pisano'! *Buon Giorino*...." Mooch said as he rose, kissing both cheeks of a hunched over, rather ghostly looking creature.

Zeto had never seen a mink quite as old or as white before in is life. He had sharp protruding features, a snout that appear almost hawkish, gaunt of face with eyeballs that protruded somewhat from their sockets, and his pelt was a mishmash of white and whiter with a full wisp of it sticking straight up on the top of his head like a Cockatoo.

"*Come sta,* Muccino Alberdini." A deep baritone voice with perfect articulation barreled from his skinny frame.

"It's been a long time, my friend. What brings you clear out here on such a cold night? Were you missing us out here at Crabby's?"

"I don't see how anyone can miss Crabby, but I miss you of course, and I miss his food. This is Zeet. Zeet, this is Agostino DeLuca, the best host, the best waiter, and he is half owner extraordinaire of this establishment."

"*Buon Giorno,* Signor DeLuca." Zeto rose formally, and extended his paw. *So "Zeet" was it? Interesting.*

"No... no... no," Agostino said as he reached out, and grabbed Zeto's body, imprisoning him in a tight bear hug.

Patting his back and kissing both cheeks he added, "Any friend of Muccino Alberdini is a friend of mine. Sit... Sit...both of you... sit and relax. Look over the menu and the specials and I'll be right back with our best house vino. I'll tell Crabby you're here Muccino. I am sure he will want to pop out to torture you.

Snow is on the way. I can feel it in my bones. These old hind legs don't move so fast anymore." He crossed himself and smiled. "I never thought I would get this old. Thought I would be young forever. But the old bones can feel snow coming... stiff as beaver tails. I'll be back with your wine."

Agostino turned and headed toward the kitchen.

"Just what I needed." Zeto said as soon as Agostino walked through the kitchen's swinging doors. "More wine. And hasn't he ever heard about personal space?"

"Listen cousin," Mooch whispered leaning over the table and tapping its red and white-checkered tablecloth with his index claw. "These are friends of mine and this is the way the other half lives--the normal other half. Many never heard of "personal space" because they are warm and friendly individuals. Bodily contact is part of showing that warmth and friendliness. If you want to learn anything about any of them from this experience, then I strongly suggest that you lighten-up a little and keep an open mind." With that, Mooch sat back in his seat, crossed both fore arms over his chest; a scowl darkened his features as he looked around the room.

Watching Mooch across the table, Zeto felt a sudden urge to laugh. "You look ridiculous sitting there pouting. Grown adult male minks do not pout."

"I am not pouting. I am brooding. There's a difference, and what looks ridiculous is that idiotic hanky stuffed half way up your nose! And really cousin, I don't think you want to know where I'd like to tell you to stick it at the moment."

"No, couz... I would. Tell me where you would like me to stick it?"

"You know Zeto," Mooch spoke between clenched teeth, "I won't tell you where to stick it because I am a gentlemink, and as a gentlemink, I do not use foul or inappropriate language in public. However, I may tell you on the way home, which may be sooner than later if you don't lighten-up. You're as stiff as a beaver tail. Someone might think you have one stuck up your...."

"Alright Muccino," Zeto cut him off, "I get the picture."

Zeto took a deep breath. He knew Mooch was right, but *that* was exactly the problem. He didn't think he knew the first thing about loosening up. With a strict autocratic upbringing; surrounded by acquaintances that were deemed *proper* by his father, he had lived most of his life in isolation.

Every move he made; every nuance was either written about or scrutinized in some fashion and anything outside that little circle in which he traveled filled him with doubt and confusion, about himself, about others and how they tended to relate to him.

He was not good at these kinds of social mechanisms with minks not of his social or economical standing; there was always some question involved in knowing where to begin, what to talk about since so few commonalities existed, so he spent his entire life avoiding situations with those outside of his own safe radius of privilege. Tonight though, through his own stupidity, he had decided to venture out into this foreignness, to learn about something he had only read about or studied and although there was a part of him that felt electrically charged, there was another equally charged side that left him dead in his tracks. He knew, if nothing more, that he had to prove something to himself tonight. He had to stay with this to its conclusion.

"Okay. You're right. I do need to lighten up. Hummm... any suggestions?"

Mooch's *brooding* frown disappeared as he turned and

smiled across at his cousin. He placed his right paw over his heart. "Just observe the master. I could have written the book on sociable behavior. It may not always be acceptable social behavior, but the book's got my name on it." At that he grinned. "Socialization 101, states that one should be themselves. I wasn't trying to insult you earlier when I said to drop the title from your name."

Mooch hesitated for a moment. "My point earlier, was that if you tell everyone who you are, then they will treat you as an outsider and you will never know what it feels like to be ordinary, a regular Joe Blow, or to be given the opportunity to understand the *common mink*. Before minks will let you in, they have to decide first that you are one of them, otherwise, you, as the Count of Ulderico, could bowl with them every Friday night at Shady Lanes, and they will never accept you into the group. That's Socialization 101 in a nutshell."

Zeto shrugged. "I suppose had I signed up for a few of those Socialization 101 courses, my total boorishness in mixing with all classes of minks would be less awkward."

"Let's just have a good time," Mooch said, notably cringing while watching Crabby make his way to their corner booth.

"AH HA! Zat skinny ol faurt zay you wooz here!" Crabby placed a bottle of some brand of wine Zeto had never heard of before on the table along with two glasses.

"I zapoze you woont ze use-u-al. I sink I drop dead on ze spot of ze heart attack if you ev-ar try zomesing new. But frum ze look of you, I sink you stick whit ze car-rot' steeks. No? Ze stom-ick look e-ven biggar' zhan ze last time I zee you. You need to loze zome weight *Signore!*"

"I do love my crab, and you're crab cakes are just too hard to resist." Mooch laughed and patted his belly for Crabby's benefit. "And it's just going to get even bigger after eating more of your scrumptious crab cakes!"

"Oh don't blow zunshine up ze ol boozhe tail. Try ze Craubmeat Marque Choux, or za Broiled Duck wit ze red peppa jhelle glauz? You olwuz in here eating ze zame ol sing. Try sumsing new for achenj."

Mooch smiled. "As tempting as that sounds, I brought my friend Zeet here for your crab cakes. Zeet this is the distinguished Signor Barouche'. He is the cook and also the other half owner of this establishment."

"I am no *kook*, I am ze chef!" Crabby spewed. "Maybe I fill you plate wit craub-*guts*, zen you can call me *kook*."

"I apologize," Mooch cajoled. "I am ignorant when it comes to the lingo dealing with a *restaurateur*. Zeet, this is Signor Barouche', our distinguished chef."

"*Buona seral*, Signor Barouche'." Zeto stood and extended his paw.

"I zee you zomewhere before. No?" Crabby probed, twisting and stretching his long neck around to where it almost touched Zeto's. He never extended his paw so Zeto sat back down. After a few seconds of patting his long claw on the side of his face, he added and pointed to Zeto, "I know I zee you before zis. A Barouche' neva forgets ze face."

"Well, Signor Barouche'… yes… you may have seen me before because I…." Mooch's hind paw slammed into his shin, making him yelp and squirm back in his seat. He closed his eyes and bent down to rub his leg while shooting lethal daggers over at Mooch. "…used to live out this way awhile back."

"No. I zee you zomwhere elze. I will sink on it. I hoope you are not as cra'-zy as your tubby frund?" Crabby looked over at Mooch and rolled his eyes. "I go now and kook. It will come to me where I hauv zeen you. And Signor Mooch, looz zom weight!"

As Crabby walked away from the table, Zeto combed his claws through the fur on his head. Perspiration beaded his brow. Why was it so hot in here?

"There was absolutely no reason for kicking me under the table like that. I swear to you, if you ever do that to me again, I will personally see that you are disemboweled and your fur made into a very large pillow for me to rest the posterior part of my anatomy on. Do you understand?"

"Don't get mad." Mooch shrugged, "It was necessary. You were about to spill the beans about whom you really are. That would have spoiled the entire purpose of this excursion. They would have treated you different, as nobility instead of one of the guys. You need to know how it feels to be treated like the rest of us. That's what this is all about, isn't it?"

"Just don't kick me like that again. I can feel a hematoma

beginning as we speak." No one had ever struck Zeto before, not even in jest.

Mooch poured them each a small glass of what appeared to be a red Burgundy. "Drink a small glass of wine." He slid it across the table. "Here. You look like you could use this."

"What I could use is a ride home." Zeto swirled the wine goblet around in his palm and then held it under his nose. He tried to sniff its bouquet. He knew he didn't have the greatest sniffer, but when it came to wine, that was a whole different ball of wax. It smelled dead in the bottle.

Zeto looked down into his glass and frowned at all the sediment floating around inside and set it back down on the table. "What is this stuff? Because this is not wine."

"Yes it is wine. Crabby and Agnostino make it. They have large barrels of it in the basement downstairs."

"It smells like vinegar, maybe rubbing alcohol and it's cloudy, not to mention the sediment floating all through it" Zeto leaned over it and took another deep sniff and pushed his glass away. "I'm not drinking that. Water will be fine."

"You will insult them if you don't drink a glass." Mooch said impatiently, while taking a deep gulp of his wine. "It won't kill you. At least try it. It really isn't bad. It's not like any wine found in your fancy wine cellars I'll grant you that, but it really is quite good considering that they do this as sort of a hobby, and then they give it away. It's free. It's their house wine and it's on the house!"

"That's because no one would actually pay good money for

this stt-stuff." Zeto took a tiny sip, sloshed it around in his mouth and swallowed. "Eeeghh... Please do not ask me to drink this. It is not fit for mink consumption! It tastes like gasoline. Do you want me to regurgitate all over the table?"

"How do you know it taste like gasoline? Have you ever tasted gasoline?" Mooch pushed the bottle to the end of the table against the wall. "Not everyone has mungo jumbo wine cellars in their castle with vintages, I can't even pronounce, dating back fifty - sixty years."

"Alright ...alright all ready... just stop talking." Zeto grabbed his wine glass and holding his breath shot it down his throat in one gulp. *"Whew... eek!"* He shook has head and exhaled deeply. "And that will be all of that!" He slammed his glass down on the table.

Mooch looked over at the contorted faces Zeto was making. He was hopeless. Utterly and completely hopeless, just sitting there with that stupid hanky dabbing at his mouth and nose. Sitting there like he had a beaver tail up his backside, no this wasn't working. He just was not cut out for any kind of normal life experience. He belonged exactly where you could always find him, up there in his ivory tower.

"Let's just get our crab cakes and go. You are not enjoying this and I am *certainly* not enjoying this...." He paused and added softly, "so let's just eat and I'll take you home."

...Zeto looked around the room. Dim lighting from one narrow taper perched in old Chianti bottles lit each table and booth.

Red and white checkerboards covered small round tables with single bud vases and several dried sprigs of holly, red berries and all, made ample winery arrangements. The hardwood floors were earth worn and there were minks everywhere. Some were dancing, most were sitting at tables and booths eating, but he noticed that all of them were paired up in some fashion or another, smiling and laughing and some were even singing.

Fun… so this is what fun looked like? He looked over at Mooch who looked miserable sulking down into his wine glass and from out of nowhere a feeling of guilt began to creep over him.

Did he actually believe in his heart that he could fit in with any of these minks? Had he given this half a chance? Did he purposely sabotage the opportunity to have fun for either one of them tonight because he believed in his heart that he was superior? That he was better than these minks?

Mooch was the one with all the advantages. He had been born on the fringes... not exactly royal; however, accepted in those circles, but no way near a commoner where he was also accepted.

He had the ability to jump around to either group. He possessed qualities that Zeto was born without and could never hope to acquire. He had been born with the natural ability to *fit in,* no matter what the situation demanded. He was a chameleon, blending in perfectly, but Mooch did not know what it was like to be constantly placed under a microscope.

He couldn't begin to understand the pressures and stress that controlled him, or maybe he did. Maybe this night's outing was

Mooch's way to show him that he could experience a without any of those pressures, that he could just mix right in there so much as a bat of an eye and be one of the guys, but the not stupid bonehead didn't understand that his place and position wa who he was. It defined him. He knew nothing else.

All things considered, outside of that place and position tiny tendrils of fear were planted, fear that would start to twirl and build around in the bottom of his belly and work their way up. He hated fear more than anything else. He hated feeling it and had worked very hard to snuff it out whenever it reared its ugly head.

Zeto leveled a look of pure sorrow. "Listen, I apologize for the way I have been acting. I will do better. I promise."

"Don't want you to be here a mite longer than need be," Mooch grumbled. "But my stomach calls."

Zeto scowled at him. "I just apologized. We will stay here as long as you like. I will act accordingly. And watch how much of that wine you are consuming, after all, you are the *designated driver*."

Mooch had never seen Zeto so green. He couldn't help feeling sorry for him. Apologizes, as scant as they were, always made Zeto appear as though he was headed to a guillotine. "My mama use to mix wine with milk in my baby bottles, so you need not worry. We both know that I can tolerate much more than you. One glass is not going to cloud my night vision nor my sense of direction. I'm a responsible Italian. One glass of wine does not inebriate us. I could drink that whole bottle and be as sober as the day I was h᷈o narrowed his eyes and watched Mooch take another

᷈ wine. "I am sure you are right; however, let's not put it to

sist."

Mooch lowered his glass from his lips and smiled sheepishly. "You're royal wish is my command." At that he gulped what was left in his wine glass straight down his throat, and turned the glass upside down on the table. His lips puckered as he hiccupped. "Water for both of us it will be...."

Agostino appeared a few minutes later with a large tray. He placed their dinners in front of them. His face tightened. "You don't care for the wine?" he asked.

"The wine is undisputedly a masterful treasure." Zeto was the first to answer. Forever the diplomat…

"Being a fanatic connoisseur of great vintages, I can say with fortitude that it is of full body and flawlessly dry, but we have decided that we could only make room for the crab cakes, but you must see to it that it is corked so that we may enjoy the rest of it at home."

"Then I will cork it for you and you can take it with you." Agostino reached across the table glowing and thanking Zeto for such a sweet praise.

"Not everyone, Signor Zeet, has your excellent taste. Believe it or not, I have had several insults leveled at me about our wine tasting like vinegar. Some minks do not have your taste or expertise in knowing a fine wine when they taste one. Thank you and enjoy your dinners."

As they watched Agostino move to another table, Zeto turned to look over at Mooch who was staring back at him.

"Don't look at me like that..." Mooch said with a big smile holding his paw up in front of him

"I'm not saying a word."

"Yes, but you were going to." Mooch picked up his napkin and laid it across his lap. "Now this is a meal fit for a king and a count too."

"I have to hand it to you, it does look delicious." Zeto looked at his plate as he unfolded his napkin and placed it over his lap. What is this?" He pointed to a small bowl with a light yellow sauce in it.

"That is the "Secret Sauce," something made with Chipotle. You'll want to lick the bowl when you're finished. Dip a little of your crab cake into it."

"And what about this?" Zeto moved it around at the end of his fork and looked over at Mooch.

"Oh, those are great. French Fried earthworms." Mooch managed to say with a mouth full of them. "They're the best!" Try them with a little of Crabby's Chipotle sauce.... Oh man, they are so good."

Zeto had never eaten an earthworm, let alone a fried one. He picked one up on the end of his fork....

"No. Use your fingers." Mooch condescendingly scolded. "Fried earthworms are considered finger-food. Didn't you ever eat them before?"

"Can't say that I have." Zeto picked one up and dipped it into the yellow condiment. *Here goes,* he thought to himself as he lifted it toward his mouth. Closing his eyes he began to chew and discovered to his great astonishment and relief that they were extremely tasty.

By some miracle of the universe Zeto felt himself beginning to relax. He let out a deep sigh, and opened his eyes to find Mooch staring at him.

"Well... what do you think?"

"Honestly, they are quite good." Zeto answered, picking up another one "I never had these before."

"See what'd I tell you?" Mooch threw his arms in the air. "This place has the best food. I told you, you'd thank me for bringing you here before the night was over."

"The night is not over Mooch." Zeto picked up his fork and broke off a piece of his crab cakes and dipped.

"I'm just a confident Neapolitan." Mooch squirted lemon over his crab cakes and picked up his fork.

"You are a *Roman*! Being born in Naples doesn't make you Neapolitan. You have spent your entire life in Rome, so I would say you are more Roman than anything else."

"Hey *viva la Italia!*" Shoving lemon drizzled crab cake into his mouth, Mooch added, "I swear sometimes when I eat here, I feel like I have died and gone to mink heaven. Nothing on God's good Earth tastes this wonderful."

I remember about a year ago, I asked Crabby what was in his "*secret sauce*" because I had never tasted anything that delicious in my life. You would have thought I cut off his *boozhe* tail. He went ba-llistic, exploding like a Skunk Bomb.... He told me he would have me permanently banned from his establishment... that it was none of my beeswax... that I was an idiot for asking such a question to any great chef.... that recipes were sacred inventions not to be shared or discussed... so on and so forth... what a crazy *demente*! That is one mink that scares me.

Mooch shook his head. "Later Agostino told me that the main ingredient was Chipotle peppers, but that he wasn't actually privy to any of Crabby's recipes. So I figured the chef must wait until everyone is sleeping and then sneak into his own kitchen and experiment? What a looney cooking genius!"

...Crab cake after luscious crab cake melted into Zeto's mouth like butter. Astonishment begat each bite. Never in his life had he ever tasted crab prepared this way. His Italian chef, Giovonni Bonifazio, considered second to none, could not on his best day perfect anything like this.

"These are absolutely incredible." Zeto finished his last bite wanting more. "Did you hear me?"

"Yeah... yeah... I heard you." Mooch said noticeably distracted.   He shifted his eyes without moving his head to something across the room.

"Zeto, don't look now, but there are two, um... really attractive females in the booth straight over and the blond one has been making goo-goo eyes at me for the last ten minutes. "Don't look over... I said! Geezooy Zeto... can't you be a little more discrete?"

Zeto turned again, in a casual manner to the right only to make eye contact with two female minks that occupied the booth directly across from them. Looking back at him, the one with natural fur smiled, while the other one, the blond one, winked and blew him a kiss.

"You mean the one with her fur dyed blond?"

"Yes. Quit staring."

"Did she just blow me a kiss?" Zeto asked incredulously.

"No, she was blowing that kiss to *me.* She's been eyeballing me all night. Isn't it obvious that she fancies me?"

Zeto turned and looked over at her again. Dyed blond fur with dark brown roots... *how interesting; never saw anything like that before.* Was he seeing correctly? There it was again. He saw it poor eyesight and all. He knew it was not a figment of his imagination.

She puckered her lips and blew a kiss dead smack center on him. He shook his head and looked up again. How bold. How brazen. Were all female minks that lived outside a court retinue as forward as this one? No one had ever introduced him to a female that made gaga eyes and blew kisses at him. He was getting a first rate education here tonight.

"Don't look," Mooch whispered from across the table, "they're coming over."

Zeto sat perfectly still, fixating on Mooch who looked up as the two approaching female minks reached their corner booth.

The blond one spoke first while the other one stood slightly behind her and giggled

"Hey ya boys. How ya'ol doin?"

"We're fff-fine thank yy-you," Mooch stammered and squeaked like a mouse. *Where did that come from?*

He paused, composed himself and tried again, "And how are you ladies tonight?" *That was better.*

"Jist fine. I'm Filomena but everyone calls me Mena and this here is Orsola. We al' call her Lalla."

"Hey there." Lalla waved and giggled some more.

"I am Muccino, but everyone calls me Mooch and this is Zeet, and everyone calls him Zeet."

"You are jist too funny." Mena batted her eyes and little peals of laughter escaped through dark red tinted lips. A thick southern twang made her speech sometimes hard to follow. "I like a mink with a sense of humor. We's pleased to make your acquaintance.

Speechless, Zeto looked up and nodded his head. Her eyes bore into him.

"We was jist wonderin if ya'ol like to join us," she

41

continued, her eyes still glued on Zeto. "We's headed fir *Road Kill*. They's havin themselves a big ol shindig tanight. Live band. Lots of dancin'. That's where we's headed."

Zeto interrupted. "Signorina Mena, may I ask you a question?"

"Sures ya can." She moved closer to where Zeto sat and looked down at him.

"Where are the two of you from? I detect an accent and I thought may be you hailed from someplace in southern Italy?"

"Nos, can't says that we is. But I do git that a bit. We's both from around these here parts. Now can I count on ya'ol to come round and meet us tanight?"

Before Zeto could make an excuse and refuse, Mooch jumped right in there.

"Ladies we would be honored to join you. Is that the place that is over near Germano's Café'?"

"That'd be it." She looked back over at Zeto. "Toodles then. We'll see ya'ol later...."

She and Lalla strutted there way to the door, but before they walked through it, she turned around and blew Zeto one big final kiss.

"Oh boy," Zeto closed his eyes and shook his head, squeezing his temples tightly with his paws. "Please tell me that you told them we would meet them as a fast way of getting rid of them? I am telling you right now that I am not going near anyplace called,

"Road Kill" especially with two slow-witted females, one mute and another that doesn't seem to have passed the third grade."

"Oh, come on, it will be fun."

"No it won't be fun and I refuse." Zeto threw his napkin on the table next to where Agostino had placed their check. "You said you were taking me out tonight, so I believe this would be yours." He pushed the check over to Mooch.

Mooch looked down at the check and reached inside his jacket for his wallet. He checked the right pocket, and then the left pocket, all the while under Zeto's watchful eye. He patted his lower pockets. "I… seem to have forgotten… my…."

"I know; you seemed to have misplaced your wallet again." Zeto rolled his eyes. "How did I know that was coming?"

"I'll pay you back. I probably left it at home on my dresser." Mooch looked over at Zeto sheepishly and added, "Don't I always pay you back?"

"No. You never pay me back. Do you even own a wallet because I have never seen this mysterious wallet that you keep misplacing." Zeto extracted a few bills, and threw them on the table. "Let's go home."

"No, we can't go home yet." Mooch looked at his watch. "The night is still young."

"Maybe it's young for you, but it's getting older by the minute for me. Come on. Take me home."

Mooch tilted his head to the left and stretched his fore arms over the top of the booth seat. "I am taking you to Road Kill first and then I will take you home. It's not every day that a female is attracted to me and I want to stop there for a little spin around the dance floor. Just one dance…. Don't shake your head *no*, hear me out. I'll get her phone number and then I will take you home."

"You are actually serious about this, aren't you?" Zeto was dumbfounded. "I can't imagine you being attracted to a female mink that dyes her fur, and her grammar? I had a hard time following her speech, and just that whole *come-on thing…*. Mooch, friend… cousin… she is not for you."

Mooch rubbed his temples, closed his eyes and then leaned his head back against the top of the leather booth. "As hard as it is for you to understand this, being that beautiful females constantly throw themselves at your feet, I have got to take what comes, when it comes. She liked me… she was attracted to me, blew me a kiss and asked me to come and dance with her. For once she liked me and not you. Do you have any idea what that feels like to never be singled out, to never be anyone's first choice? I just want one dance Zeto, one stupid dance and her phone number, that's all I ask… and then we can head back home."

Zeto became alarmed at what he was about to do, but how could he refuse him after that? "If that's really what you want Mooch, then far be it from me to refuse you." He couldn't think of anything else to say. "One dance and her phone number and that's it, right?

"Right Zeto. And thanks…."

Zeto would never understand Mooch, not if he lived a thousand years. What compels a mink to chase after females like that? The last thing that Zeto wanted to do was to go to a place called *Road Kill*.

Who would name a place *Road Kill* and better yet, what kind of minks went there? It didn't sound good. He suddenly felt very tired. He would take his life and the way he lived over anything that he had witnessed thus far tonight. He wanted his nice soft, warm bed, that's what he wanted. He yawned as they made their way to Crabby's exit carrying a corked bottle of extremely bad wine, which he planned to pitch as soon as they started down the ridge. One more stop…. He supposed that wouldn't be so bad.

45

Chapter Three
Road Kill

Several small tributaries from the Tiber twisted and looped around natural fords and small tracts of land. Flooding, in areas near *Ponte Cestio* were frequent in the spring when torrential rainfall saturated water basins and made the earth soggy and difficult to travel upon, but tonight the earth was dry, the wintry air, crisp; frozen leaves crunched underfoot.

Thirty minutes later Mooch could see a flashing neon blue sign in the distance. Zeto saw nothing. Road Kill was straight ahead, located on the other side of Jamberetti's Vineyard across the way from Germano's Café. It was nestled in the foothills of the Apennines under an awning of naked trees.

Gnarled roots and deformed branches gave it an ominous appearance. Spooky. In the middle of nowhere, Road Kill looked to be nothing more than an oversized den of some sort, which had been abandoned by a rather massive animal, and tunneled next to the bank of a small running creek.

Zeto winced as his vision cleared. *Seedy* was the only word he could formulate to describe it. He dreaded the thought of entering such a place. Dingy lanterns illuminated the entryway every few meters and some type of music he could not name blasted out into the night's stillness. A group of about six or seven minks mingled around the front door and from what he could see as he and Mooch moved closer toward them, made his heart suddenly thump a little faster in his chest.

One look at them told Zeto all he needed to know. At that moment, more than anything, he wanted to turn, and throttle Mooch for bringing him to such a place. How did he know it was going to be like this? A place that most sane minks would go out of their way to avoid, he was walking into and on his own free will. How much sense did that make? The minks standing around in an almost perfect semicircle were all males and they quietly eyeballed Zeto and Mooch as they made their approach.

They all possessed scraggly whiskers braided down the front of their chests and Italian flag bandannas covered some of their heads. Skulls and crossbones garnished all their leather vests. He could make out the word "Dragon" on the back of one leather jacket with a fire spewing green dragon coiling up the back and around the sleeve of one of the biggest minks he had ever seen. Lord help them!

"Well... well... well, lookey what we got here boys," one especially menacing looking mink said, slapping the back of the mink standing next to him. "We got ourselves a couple of fancy-pancy city boys ... a gen-u-ine pretty boy and a pudgy little ol' roly-poly. Ain't everyday ya sees sumthin like that in these here parts! And check out those duds."

Their snickers almost stopped Zeto in his tracks, but together he and Mooch continued under their gruff scrutiny.

"Excuse me gentleminks," Zeto finally breathed out, he stood before them with his hands shoved in his pockets.

"I ain't seen no gentlemink folks round here." An intense loathing reverberated from a hulking looking brute missing a few front teeth. He looked around his group. "You seen any gentleminks round here Vito?"

Another one of them, a wary looking Vito, Zeto supposed, with shifty eyes, gangly and tall, stared straight into Zeto's face as he turned and spit, "Nope. Can't say as I do. We eats 'em fir breakfast friend."

But Zeto was not deterred. Although he had absolutely no past experience in defusing situations with these types of individuals, he knows if he backs down and slinks away, he and Mooch will be pushed and bounced around and it was seven against two, so he gathered all the diplomatic finesse he had brought to many political and social tables and dove right in.

"But we heard there was a great band playing here tonight and yes, we are from the city, and being from the city, we rarely get the chance to hear well-written folk or country music. So we came all this way to listen because we heard there were some great musicians here tonight playing some really good music."

"Well ya all came ta the right place cause we's it." The mink with the bulked-up biceps and dragon decal said as he quieted the rest of his companions down with a stone cold glare. "Don't pay no mind to these here fools, theys jist foolin wit ya. We's *The Backbiters*. We's jist takin a little break right now. What ya all hearin' in there is jist a few nasty ol' tuned fiddles makin' a whole lotta noise. Go on now, git inside and have yerselves a hoopdeedo."

49

"Thank you." Zeto began to breathe again. "We will be looking forward to listening to your music."

Both Zeto and Mooch made there way passed them and through the doorway when a loud burst of laughter erupted from right behind them.

Mooch stopped and as he began to slowly turn around, Zeto snatched his arm tightly and pulled him toward him. With a deadly calm voice, he whispered into his ear.... "If they do not pulverize you before this night is over, I will. Go find your female, have your dance and get your phone number and then you had better be ready to leave this mountain sewer so *HELP ME GOD!*"

Mooch nodded, a pro at knowing when to keep his mouth shut, and disappeared through a throng of rough-looking minks that were jammed together like canned sardines.

Zeto had never seen such a crowd in his life. This appeared to be a place right out of some Stephen Kinkmink novel. No one would ever believe him. *Where did all these minks come from* he wondered? Did they slink down from the Apennines every Saturday night from Hillbilly Road? Was he witnessing some kind of congenital aberration? He had never seen anything like the faces that watched him as he slowly passed by. Mooch had hit the nail right on the proverbial head. Zeto had surely led a sheltered life because he couldn't begin to make this stuff up. Nothing in his imagination could have prepared him for this. The minks that gathered here were just too outrageous to be believable.

Smaller lanterns hung from the walls inside and brightened the place. His eyesight was clearing, unobstructed but ironically, this was one time in his life where he would not have minded being totally blind. A large stage had been erected from mottled wood crates and one banjo and four fiddlers plucked away, but from what he could see no one seemed to be paying them much mind. Minks were everywhere. Some were on a circular dance floor doing some kind of shuffle thing with their feet, which did not look like any dancing he had ever encountered. But the way this night was going, anything was possible.

This place made Crabby's smell like a perfume factory. He dabbed at his nose with his crumpled handkerchief. An unpleasant odor he could barely detect filled the cramped and smoke-filled room. Female minks with painted faces, rouged cheeks and cherry lips and fur, colors he had never imagined, stared at him as he walked by.

He nodded and walked on never giving any one of them the impression that this place and everyone in it offended him. He leaned against the wall, trying to see where Mooch had scurried off to, when a female mink with a large-set smile, all teeth and big purple painted lips stood before him like a circus clown. He gazed down at her and could not help but to notice that her tail was wrapped around her neck and was decorated with giant yellow and purple bows. She lifted her front paw up and twirled one of the ribbons with her claw.

"Howdy there," she said as she gave him the *once over.*

"Hello," he answered brusquely, feeling her squeeze herself into his personal space. He frowned and maneuvered himself slightly back and to the left.

"I noticed ya all from clear over there." She turned and pointed to the other side of the room. Yelling over the music she added wide-eyed, "I knows I never seen ya all here before, cause I'd a never forgot a face like that. What's your name cutie pie?"

Did he just hear her right? Did she just refer to him as *"cutie pie?"* This night was becoming more bizarre by the moment.

He cleared his throat. "Zeet."

"Well howdy there Zeet." Her pudgy painted face stared up at him. "I knows you was a gentlemink the minute I seen those spensive clothes." She ran her paw over the lapel of his coat and touched the Gucci stripes of the muffler that hung from his neck. "A lady mink like myself, we notices things as such. I always says that a mink with a sense of designer fashion is a mink fir me. Hows bout you and me we git out there and shows them all how to dance?"

"I am sorry Signorina…."

"Ohhh, lordy me," she giggled as she pounded her head, "I'm jist a little ol' donkey head now ain't I… my name is Luita, but ya all can call me Lulu."

"Well, Signorina Lulu, I am afraid that I am only waiting for a friend who should be here momentarily. But I thank you."

"What's the matter Mr. Zeet," Lulu said crossing her arms in front of her, an expression of annoyance cascaded over her face, "ain't I good enough fir your rich ol' blood?"

"I assure you Signorina that had I more time it would be my pleasure to dance with you, but as I was saying…."

"Oh...Yoohoo… Signor Zeety," a voice came from his right. He could not imagine this night getting any worse, but there it was. Waving her tail as she approached and moving rapidly toward them was Mena and in a blink of an eye he could see where this was all going. A tiny tick began at the base of his jaw.

"Is this here the "*friend*" you say you was *waitin* fir?" Lulu asked in open amazement?

"Luita Lea Marie," Mena walked up and twirled her arm through Zeto's. "I do believe this here is *my* date and you need to skedaddle."

"Well you listen here Miss Up Fluff," she moved in closer to Mena, "I knows fir a fact that yous almost spoken fir." She turned and looked at Zeto. "She's got herself a male and he's in the band that'll be comin' on in a few minutes an he is a *kind* mink, the *kind* ya all need to run from when he gits mad. And nothing' makes him madder or meaner then seeing his Mena flirtin' with another mink."

"Now you listen here yo ol' weasel face," Mena snuggled closer into Zeto who found it almost impossible to disentangle himself from her arms, arms that seemed to tighten like steel bands. "I do as I please and it ain't none of yer business. So keeps yer big 'ol trap shut and yer skanky ol' nose outta my affairs!"

"Ladies, please…." Zeto tried to remove Mena's arm from around him, slowly prying her forepaw loose which was digging into his fur.

"I came here tonight Miss Mena because Mooch wanted to dance with you and he is out there somewhere looking for you." He pointed toward the masses of minks mingling in the center of the room. "As a gentlemink, I could not possibly wound a fellow minkmate, not to mention a very dear relative and friend by dancing with someone he found so very attractive that he traveled all this way to see."

"Ya mean that ol' tubby one ya ol' was with at Crabby's?" Mena's paws dropped to her hips. "The super-sizer"?

"Mooch. Remember. His name is Muccinio Alberdinni."

"Oh I ain't got no hankering fir him. It'd be you, Signor Zeet that I wants to know better." She reached out to grab his wrist, but Zeto was quicker and moved out of her reach.

"Well there now Miss Up Fluff, seems to me that this here Romeo don't got no *hankering* fir you, so if ya all jist excuse us we'll be on our way." Lulu grabbed Zeto's arm and started to drag him across the room.

Zeto made a weak attempt to pull his arm out of her grasp, but she hung on. This was becoming an absolute *nightmare!* He tried to concentrate on where to find Mooch. He inclined his head and loomed above the minks milling around searching desperately in a fog of faces for the one he was either going to kiss or kill. They almost made it to the other side of the room, when Mena caught up with them, and yanked the fur on the back of Lulu's head....

"Signor Zeety," she called, an air of seething rage

resounded, palpable to everyone around so that the small corner of the room suddenly began to grow very quiet. "This little ol' Jezebel here is a liar and a...."

Before she could say another word, Lulu sprang, shoving Mena back and grabbing at her throat. Without thinking, Zeto grabbed and pulled both females apart.

"Ladies... ladies... please," he separated them, but they struggled against his arms to claw at one another.

"Ladies!" Zeto held fast, using all the strength he had to restrict their movement. "Please... you are both drawing attention to yourselves in a most unbecoming way and there is no need for all this. As lovely as you both are, you must realize that the rest of the male mink population in here or for that matter, anywhere, would give all their canines for one dance with either of you. You both need to calm down."

He stalled for a second before adding, noticing that both females were slowly easing in their struggles to free themselves from his clasp to get to each other.

"I find both of you extremely, incontrovertibly attractive, but I am already spoken for. I am nearly engaged and I do apologize if I gave either one of you an incorrect impression, but the truth is that I am one foot from the altar...."

It was about then that several loud shrieks interrupted his train of thought and curiously he turned to see where the commotion was coming from. The mob parted like the Red Sea, and in the middle of it was Mooch speeding toward him, hind legs moving as he had never seen or thought possible. Behind him and traveling at about the same kilometers per hour was the fire breathing Dragon King, black jacket and all, biceps flailing out in front of him, teeth snapping, outrage contorting his face.

Mooch barely had time to snatch Zeto away before, Lulu stepped forward and with a quick lift of her chin, she put her hind leg out in front of her and tripped the Dragon monster that was trailing after them and down he went.

"Thank you Signor Zeet!" he heard her yell…. "Them was the nicest words anyone has ever said to me… now GIT!!!!"

…Only by divine intervention did they make it outside of the bottomless pit, and clutching onto Mooch's back, they tore through the woods until they could no longer hear the stampeding gang behind them.

He never knew Mooch had it in him, and a part of him was extremely impressed. "I think you can slow down now Mooch." Zeto said, but Mooch kept up the pace. "Mooch, I said you can slow down now."

But Mooch kept running, turning a deaf ear, his fore and hind legs moved at a speed Zeto would never have thought possible at his cumbersome weight. He clung to his back seeing only blackness.

"Mooch… Mooch… please slow down, you're going to have a heart-attack."

"Are they gone?" Mooch whispered plunging behind the

trunk of a very large tree. His breathing was labored; a white froth rimmed his mouth.

"Listen to me. You need to sit. Calm down and sit here, no right here," Zeto pointed to a soft clump of leaves piled around the base of the trunk. He tried to make his voice smooth, consoling.

"Okay. That's it. Sit all the way back. Take a deep breath and rest your head back and close your eyes. Close them. You're going to be okay Mooch or else I am going to kill you."

With closed eyes, Mooch chuckled. "I **thought** we were both goners."

"Just relax. We're fine." Zeto sat down next to him, shadows loomed all around him but he could see **nothing** distinct. He could make out the front of Mooch's face and saw that he had his head rested back against the tree, but that his eyes had opened. "What exactly happened back there?"

Mooch kept his voice low, sniffing the air and glancing around. "Do you think they're still on our trail?"

"You're asking me? You're the scent expert. I am the one with no ability to scent others or to see in the dark. Do you smell any of them?"

Mooch sniffed the air again. "Not right now, but judging from the sounds and scents at one point they were snapping at our heels and closing in, and I think there was more than just that dragon maniac freak of nature."

Mooch grabbed Zeto by both shoulders. "Oh …I never thought…mmm-maybe they're out there just toying with us or setting up some kind of ttt-trap or camouflaging themselves somehow ready to sss-spring out at us at any given moment. Oh jeez... and just the two of us, out here in this wilderness...with all of them. You remember the movie *Deliverance* don't you...?"

"Don't be silly Mooch. You're letting your imagination get the best of you. No one is out **there** lurking. You would be able to pick up some type of foreign scent, wouldn't you?"

"I don't know. I never **had** to test my ability." He leaned back, closed his eyes and sniffed the **air** again. "My instincts say *no*, but I was never in this position in my entire life so I have no way of knowing for certain."

"I thought you told me that you could scent at up to three kilometers away."

"Well, I may have exaggerated a little on the distance, but I do have a great sniffer, but like I said, I never had to really put it to the test. At the moment I think we are safe, but I'm going to need therapy after this. We're talking some real psychoanalysis stuff. I mean it. I don't know if I have the strength or lung capacity to dodge another bullet if they come back for us again. Man-O-Gee... what then? I was so scared that I am afraid I left quite a pungent aroma back there... I couldn't help it. It just let loose, so there is a bit of my odor lurking back there with them and maybe they're picking up my scent as we speak."

"You mean you *released* yourself? We're talking fright gland release? No way. Even *I* would have been able to smell *that*."

"...I couldn't help it. It just slipped out and I couldn't control it."

"***Skunks*** can't control that. You're a mink. We are built for more stress endurance of the adrenal flow before we release that."

"And that coming from the mouth of a mink that has never been in a position of fear in his entire life because he has hundreds of guards constantly surrounding and protecting him. Jeezooy Zeto, give me a break will you? I'm running as fast as I can with you hanging on my back. It's not something I'm proud of but it happened."

"Okay... just forget about it...." Zeto whispered. "Tell me exactly what happened back there in that squalid hole you took me to. I still have that... that smell on my clothes. But I have got to hand it to you Mooch, you sure showed me what I good time I have been missing all my life. I could have been rubbing elbows with all those crud-eating mountain minks and having myself a *'hoopdedo'*. I long to go back to that bluegrass slum hole you dragged me into. Maybe next weekend? Is this what I have been missing in my entire life Mooch? Is this what *life in motion* looks like? Are these the experiences that you spoke of that were to give me inner growth?"

"Alright." Mooch began, "You can stop with the histrionics. I get your drift."

"So tell me. What happened?"

Mooch stuck his head down between his legs and sniffed. "No odor. At least I don't think I dragged it here."

"Oh for God sake, Mooch, answer my question. You took us to the backdrop of the Apennines. What did you do to that oversized Neanderthal that made him act like a rabid dog? I think he was actually frothing at the mouth...."

"I'm really not sure what I did." Mooch scratched his head. "They all came back in from outside, all seven of those nasty bearded mountaineers to play their next set of that bluegrass fiddle stuff and the big one, the dragon king, stops me and asks me real nice if I was enjoying myself, you know, going out of his way to be friendly and all. I told him that I had met a female at Crabby's and that she was really coming onto me, you know blowing me kisses and twitching her nose."

"Oh, I can see where this is going...."

"How do you know anything? When I saw you, it looked to me as if Mena and that other female were fighting over you!"

"Just get back to the story."

"That's about it."

"And he went crazy over that?"

He hesitated for a second. "Well... I guess there's a little more.

"I am sure there is. I'm listening."

"Well as I was saying, I sort of implied that she you know, was coming on to me, with the kiss blowing and winking and that thing she did with her nose, and he asked me who she was that maybe he could help me out because he knew just about everyone in, *"these here parts,"* and so I told him her name was Filomena, but that she told us that everyone called her Mena and with no forewarning, he went berserk —rabid --let out this loud snarl and hissed at me so close to my face, that I could smell the stank on his breath. That's about when he went for my neck with his teeth and believe you me they were all there and now here we are."

Zeto sat shaking his head. "That was Mena's, oh what did Lulu call him, "*her spoken one*." You were basically telling her boyfriend that his female wanted…."

"Stop okay? I get it…. I get it!"

"Yes, Mr. Alberdinni I was hoping you would get it. You almost got us killed over a female that already had a mate."

"I told you to drop it. I get the picture. And now, I realize that all those air born kisses and winks were intended for you. Once again cousin, you had them falling at your feet."

"Let's just get out of here." Zeto stood, brushing leaves from him and suddenly found himself very tired, homesick. He missed his bed. "Which way is home."

Mooch took a deep breath. "Back the same way we came."

Crouched over, Zeto gave Mooch a knowing glance and turned around in the direction they had come. A wave of frustration gathered like a ball of lava in the pit of his stomach.

"You mean back to Hillbilly Hollow? Back to Lunatic Lane? You have got to be kidding! I am seriously thinking of dragging you back there and letting them finish you off! You got us into this mess! Now *YOU* find a way to get us out!"

Mooch stood up and looked around. "I know my way

around these woods like the back of my paw. No need to get excited. …I can't think when you're yelling at me like that.

There is a way around, but it will just take a little longer and I mean longer because I am petering out fast. These hind legs have taken a beating tonight and they don't want to move, they feel like jelly-balls so we are going to have to walk back and I mean walk back slowly."

"Come on." Zeto grabbed Mooch's tail and they began to move. "Remember that I'm back here, so *try* not to have any more *accidents*."

"That's between us." Mooch recoiled, his face grave. "As a gentlemink, I expect it to stay that way.…"

Zeto and Mooch moved through the forest at a moderately slow clip saying very little to one another. They were both exhausted. Road Kill was now far behind them.

It was the first time Zeto had ever heard the sounds of the night deep in the woods. He could hear all sorts of woodsy sounds; some left over frogs started to croak, their sound growing louder as they walked onward. The forest spoke to them in one universal language, the language of nature, a language Zeto had never heard nor cared to understand before and he found it beautiful if not a bit eerie.

He had never felt vulnerability this intense in his life if this was what he was feeling. Eyesight was not among the strongest attributes for any mink, but his was literally nonexistent. He wondered if there were stars in the sky. He knew there was no moon. Earlier Mooch had told him that the sky must be cloud covered because it was as dark as pitch, and he supposed Mooch saw no moon either.

He wondered about all the predators out there roaming around, hunting during this time of night. The thought gave him the willies. His entire life, his mother talked about predators. From minky to full adult minkhood he listened to horrific stories about the Barn Owls and subspecies of wolves and foxes.

He felt regret that he had never learned to protect himself, but then why would he ever have to? Not any of his family predecessors had learned self-protection skills because none of them were stupid enough to get themselves stuck in the situation he was now in.

The entire night was insane from the onset and he had been insane in agreeing to it. His male ego had been challenged and a brainless decision was made which was completely out of character for him.

He flourished on goal oriented planning, methodical precision specifics with all decisions and judgment calls held under different degrees and levels of scrutiny. He would remember this night and its lesson. If he lived to be a hundred, he would never make another rash spur of the moment decision again.

Who needed spontaneity? Spontaneity was for minks that had too much time on their hands or not enough intelligence in their brains. Well laid out ledgers and plans with detailed schedules made him tick; challenges of the mind... that's what life was all about.

His life would continue in the same vein once he got back home--*if they got home.*

He had gone from Puccini's, *Madam Butterfly* and Verdi's *Aida*, to some weird kind of country bluegrass in one night. He had grown from this experience, grown to know that he liked his life just the way it was and would not change one thing about it.

The sounds of water sprang up not far from where they walked. The night's quietness began to peel away. Zeto could feel a sudden drop in the temperature as they continued, a cold blast of winter air.

Mooch stopped in the weeds in silence, tired and looked at another tributary of the Tiber River, this one with a wider span. Zeto dropped his tail, feeling a flicker of dread. His body was still in hyper vigilant mode.

"I know you can't see this, but we have come to another tributary, oh I'd say about 80 to 100 meters across. But, you know, I don't remember this being here," said Mooch.

"Are we lost?" Zeto could feel his blood pressure rising.

"No." Under a sliver of moonlight that appeared sporadically, Mooch swallowed hard as the river beyond them opened in the clearing. "I just don't remember this channel being this wide."

"You don't remember a lot of things these days do you?"

"No cousin, I suppose I don't. But I think there is another way around it. We may have to walk a while longer to get around, but what the hey, look how long we have been walking already. I bet I lost five pounds tonight."

"Let's just swim across and save on time."

He could see Mooch's eyes grow wide; his scruffy fur was matted and covered with dirt and plant debris.

"I think we would be better off going around it or just camping out here until morning."

"Not an option. I don't plan on making myself a sitting target for some hungry owl or fox food. I say we go across."

Mooch sat on the bank and rested his head in his hands. "Not an option."

Zeto sighed. "I really don't want to ask this question. But I am going to ask it anyway. ...Why Mooch? Why can't we cross the channel?"

"Because, ...I ...I c-c-can't swim...."

"You mean you can't swim with me on your back? You told me yourself that you had the water skills of an otter when it came to swimming so you have to be a pretty strong swimmer and 100 meters is nothing to an otter. I don't see what the problem is if I am on your back or hanging on your tail."

"I said I can't sss-swim period. Comprende?"

"WHAT DO YOU MEAN YOU CAN'T SWIM PERIOD?" Zeto snapped, hating himself for losing his temper, but he was cold, tired, and blind. At this very minute all his patience was zapped out into a vortex. He wanted to get home. He wanted an hour-long hot shower and more than anything else, he wanted his nice big warm bed.

"I may have exaggerated a little on my water and swimming abilities."

"*You can swim down to the depth of 100 meters and dive from 20 meters into any open body of water. Our hind legs are webbed for the purpose that God intended.*" Zeto mimicked. "I can't believe this. I really can't believe this!" He sat down far enough away from Mooch to prevent himself from strangling him, and buried his head in his paws.

"I'm really sorry Zeto for getting us into this mess.... I know I told you I was a great swimmer, but truth be known... I sink like a ton of bricks and believe me, I have tried. Maybe my weight has something to do with it.

My father gave me a few lessons before he absconded with all that money from the Royal Treasury and disappeared, when I was still a minky, but after a few attempts he gave up, said I was hopeless.... He yelled at my mother for feeding me too much and making me fat...said it was no wonder I could hardly move. He said I defied physics...that any mink with as much blubber as I had should float like a buoy--never sink. ...He said I was useless.

I really did try. I wanted to make him proud of me, so I went out a few times on my own, but almost drown. I feel bad about this. I am really sorry."

Zeto let out a long sigh and his head fell down on his chest.

"Oh, this is just great Mooch…." The sound of his voice was almost a whisper.

He picked his head back up and looked over at Mooch whose face was also buried in his paws. "As much as I would like strangle you right now, I have to tell you that I was impressed tonight with the speed in which you can navigate. Not that I don't want to kill you at this very moment for getting us into this jam, but I have to admit …*you can move!*"

"Really?" Mooch smiled. Even though Zeto could not see it, he could hear the smile in Mooch's voice. "I *was* pretty fast wasn't I?"

"Well, we can't just sit here and do nothing… we must persevere. You said there was a way around. Is that the truth or is that another one of your *little exaggerations*?"

"No, there is a way around and I am feeling a little stronger now. But I sure could use something to eat. I burned a lot of calories running. I wonder if I leaned over just a little and waited, a nice big juicy frog might happen by. They are almost out of season you know?"

Zeto was appalled. "You would eat a frog… *raw*?"

"I have eaten many a raw frog in my day. I only get frog legs lightly breaded, sautéed in butter, garlic and fresh parsley when I eat with you. Actually they are better raw. They are very juicy with the organs intact and…."

"Alright, stop that." Zeto's stomach turned. "If you must do so, do it in private because not only do I not want to *see* it, which would be extremely distasteful, but neither would I want to *hear* it, which would be even more distasteful. Go ahead. I'll just sit here and wait, but go somewhere else and gorge yourself if you must."

Mooch was already moving. "I'll just mosey on down the bank a bit... I'll be right back."

Zeto sat in high weeds. This was a first. Sitting in weeds. *Weeds*! He shook his head. Will wonders never cease? Being a natural born pessimist, he wondered what else would possibly go wrong before the night's end?

He sank further back into high weeds trying to keep hidden from the keen vision of overhead predators. He thought about Mooch out there eating raw frogs and cringed again, but then a new thought entered his head, what if something happened to Mooch? Mooch was his one-way ticket home. If something should happen to him he could possibly die out here. Alone. No one would ever know what had happened to him. His bones would be carried and scattered by wild animals, never to be found again. He would be lost forever. Finished.

His mother would be crushed. She would never know why he never came home. She had spent her life covering him in bubble wrap and all for what? So he could die out here alone, never to be seen or heard from again...?

At the thought, the blood rushed from his head and his heart started pounding in his chest. *Thump... thump... thump.* He could not imagine being attacked, an animal's large sharp teeth and claws sinking into his flesh. Ripping into his throat…. *Thump… thump… thump.* His heart raced. He couldn't seem to catch his breath, his heart sped up and he couldn't get enough oxygen to his brain. *…Thump… thump… THUMP! Claws digging around inside him….*

"Okay, I'm back." Mooch plopped down beside him. "Hey, what's the matter with you? You look like you've seen a ghost. Are you alright?"

Zeto tried to get his vocal chords to cooperate and to quell his trembling body, and breathe. "I'm fine." He sighed and inhaled deeply. "Just sitting here waiting for an owl to swoop down and eat me alive."

"Listen friend, we are going to be alright. Now that my belly is full, I find I have gained much needed strength. Like I said, I must have burned a lot of calories back there. Do you think I look any thinner?"

"Please Muccino. I just want to get back home."

"Okay, grab on and let's go for a ride."

Zeto took Mooch's tail and swiftly they moved down a path that winded along the river's bank. The river moved along the tree line. The wind picked up speed, blowing colder temperatures off its surface. They traveled much faster, more determined in their steps for about two kilometers when a burst of odor permeated Mooch's nostrils.

"Holy Moly… I can't believe this!"

"Believe what?" Zeto noticed they were slowing down.

"Crayfish."

"What do you mean *crayfish*?" Mooch had stopped moving and was sniffing at the air again.

"Over there..." He pointed and started in the direction. "Can't you smell them?"

Zeto tagged after him, still clutching his tail with one paw and pulling his coat more tightly around him with the other. "I don't think it's a good idea to stray from this path. Let it go, Mooch. You just finished eating."

"Yeah, but crayfish? Come on Zeto, I can't pass this up and they're right there. *Look*."

Zeto tried to see, but that was impossible; however, he did detect a slight fishy odor. They walked over crunchy frost covered leaves and into a corner by a tree, not far from the river's bank. In the corner Mooch bent down to pick up a crayfish; there was several of them strewn around. All he needed to do was to break them open. As soon as Zeto followed him in, they both heard a faint clanking sound and then a click. ...*a very distinct click.*

"What was that? Zeto said.

"I don't know." Mooch answered.

They both turned toward the direction of the sound and found themselves unable to move outward, as though some invisible barrier prevented their forward movement. Zeto felt through dried leaves at very fine wire mesh.

"WE'RE IN A TRAP OF SOME KIND!" Zeto yelled,

actually screamed.

"We can't be," Mooch answered pushing against a firm leaf-covered wall. Together they used their claws to scrape at the leaves until what stood before them filled them with a deep, bone-chilling dread. Their hearts stopped and as if their brains suddenly became one functioning unit, they both began pushing and shoving using both fore and hind legs together, driving, blowing, attacking, but the steel wired door would not budge.

They exerted every ounce of energy trying to get the door to open, tried using their teeth to bite at the steel wire, claws to rip it apart, but nothing worked. They spent the rest of the night not speaking just rushing at it, impaling themselves against it, until dawn started to creep up over the horizon.

They sat across from each other, and for the first time Zeto could see everything around him. The woodlands seen through the inside of a steel mesh cage. The floor and walls had been covered in leaves and the crayfish in the corner, the bait. He looked over at Mooch's miserable face and he wanted to pound him, slug him, --smash his face in.

"Zeto, I am so..." Mooch started to say.

"Do not say a word." Zeto cut him off, enunciating each word slowly. "Do not say one word because I will not be able to control myself. So... just... shut... your... mouth...."

Suddenly they heard footsteps crunch underfoot, followed

by movement. Up they went. They clutched the wire floor of the trap so they wouldn't tumble over.

"Well Hiya in there little fellas," A large round adult male face stared in at them. "I knew you couldn't resist my crayfish… Works all the time.

My name is Giuseppe Tucci and I am going to be your new best friend for the next couple of months. I am taking you both to; well think of it as a kind of spa-resort." He laughed at that.

Mooch and Zeto sat glassy eyed as they were being carried away.

Giuseppe grinned like a Cheshire cat. "Everyone calls me crazy for talking to my little furry friends, but all of you have been so good to me. I believe in friendliness. When my wife isn't looking, I also talk to my plants."

They were moving with a little swing action and Zeto was becoming sick to his stomach, motion sickness was another new sensation that he would have been much happier not knowing he was susceptible to.

"That doesn't sound so bad," Mooch tried to smile. "I could use a few days at a spa."

"You idiot." Zeto seethed. *"You stupid… stupid idiot.* He's not taking us to a spa. He's taking us to a farm. A mink farm and *we both know what happens there…."*

* * * *

Chapter Four

Tucci's Mink Farm

Contessa Arabella opened beveled glassed French doors leading out from her bedroom unprepared for the blast of frozen air that hit her face. She walked outside and began to pace back and forth across an alabaster balcony made of limestone, looking out and over her son's vast stretch of land.

Still, no sign of him. She closed her eyes and sighed. Her heart knew that something was wrong--very wrong. He would never make her worry like this. She always knew where he was. She realized he was a grown adult mink, but he respected and loved her enough to mention his plans. He was never secretive about his comings and goings. She could not have asked for a more thoughtful son.

Last night, he simply walked out the front door and vanished. He left without taking any security with him and had yet to return. *"Why Zeto? Why now?"* She had been up half the night, asking herself that same question over and over.

The security that had been posted outside, after she had questioned and re-questioned them, said that he specifically expressed his desire to be left alone. They said they were *commanded* not to follow him under any circumstance, and she was angry with them, with all of them, for not following him regardless of his wishes. They had always been paid well to protect this family, and they had failed in their duty to do just that.

She could not understand Zeto's request to venture out on his own, especially at night, since from childhood he had never set one toe-claw outside these palace walls without being accompanied by some type of security. How many of their kind left their homes, never to be seen or heard from again? Too many to think about.

She walked over to the other side of the balcony. The stone under her hind paws was freezing but she felt nothing, not even the strong winter gale that brought giant snowflakes with it. Her Zeto was out there somewhere with Muccino, alone, with no protection whatsoever. She had sent an army of them out to track their scents, if the recent robust snow hadn't buried it by now.

She knew she had to calm herself down. She held her fore paws in front of her and watched as they trembled. She was of no use to anyone this way. She had called for her brother, Zeto's Uncle Angelo, who was coming all the way from Montenerodomo in the Chieti providence, where many of her family still lived.

He had a long way to come, but he never failed her since her beloved Sal had passed several years ago. Zeto, whom he loved like the son he never had, was his one and only nephew, and there was nothing that Angelo wouldn't do for Zeto, or for her.

...She turned from the baluster and walked into her bedroom and closed the French doors behind her. She moved slowly over to her nightstand and picked up his picture and kissed it and began to tear-up. *"My son. My lovely darling son... where are you? Why haven't you come home to your mama? I love you my darling. Please come home to me."* She couldn't lose him too. She placed his portrait back on the slick marble surface and turned and fell upon her bed and cried....

Mooch was picking up the scents of many minks, both male and female coming from all different directions. Their cage rocked back and forth, but both he and Zeto, still holding onto the steel mesh, sat as stiff as quarry stones. He knew they were in the back of a human motor vehicle. He looked around at where they were being taken and dread, a dread that spread like a slow seeping molasses moved through him. Zeto would not look at him, let alone speak to him. He tried several times to engage him in conversation, but his expression excised any further attempt at that.

When Zeto did glance over at him, his eyes were filled with disgust, anger. Mooch couldn't blame him. All of this fell upon his shoulders. He really screwed up this time. He could feel his entire body shivering. He rubbed his forearms and paws, but still couldn't get warm. His body shook, *...so cold*, the kind of cold that settled deep in the bone. Mooch felt as though not a single strand of fur remained on his body, and now his teeth began to chatter. He closed his eyes feeling himself tremble and a heaviness weighed upon his chest. For some reason his airway seemed blocked. *Couldn't ...get ...enough ...air.* He took a deep gulping breath.

He concentrated on breathing in and breathing out, his lungs filling and expelling, moving, rushing, but desperately lacking in oxygen. *Couldn't ...breathe.*

He could hear this terrible sound begin from somewhere, some high piercing frantic squeal only to realize that it was coming from him and that he could feel himself losing control, control of his fear glands and he knew that Zeto would kill him for his lack of control while trapped in this cage with him and would forever hate him for this weakness.

"Mooch stop it!" Zeto gripped his shoulders and shook him. "Please, Mooch." He shook him again.

Mooch still gasped trying to breathe… *huff, huff, huff.*

"Mooch stop it *I tell you*!" Zeto shook him harder.

"Huff… huff… huff…."

"Mooch…." His paw swung hard and landed across the side of his face. Mooch was momentarily stunned, and gulped hard as air returned to his lungs. He brought his paw up to touch his still stinging cheek.

"Listen to me," Zeto hissed in his face. "We are not going to get out of this mess if you fall apart on me. We are going to have to think, and think clearly. Look at me."

Zeto was breathing hard. He clutched both lapels of Mooch's jacket and shook him. "I said, ***listen to me***! We are both going to be coats, hats, scarves, stoles and oil unless you snap out of it and start to think clearly. We have to remain calm so that we can carefully study the environment we are about to enter. You have got to stay glued. I cannot deal with what is about to happen to us and you going rabid! Are you listening to me Mooch?"

Mooch gave a weak nod.

"Okay then." Zeto let go of the material clutched between his paws. "When we reach this farm, this ranch, he has plans to place us somewhere; hopefully we will not be separated, but if we are, I will try to seek you out and you will have to keep it together and try to seek me out. But listen to me Mooch, because we may not get another opportunity. You cannot lose control of yourself in there because we are about to meet a whole lot of other minks that are in our same dire situation, some even worse, and we have to gather as much information as possible.

The more information and knowledge we can obtain in there, the better and no one will want to be around you if your fear continues to control your glands. Are you listening to me Mooch? Are you understanding me?"

Mooch nodded again.

He looked his cousin in the eye. "Somehow we will find a way. I don't have the answers, but gathering as much knowledge is our only hope. I am sure that by now my mother has sent scores of guards and higher-ranking security out to pick up our scents but if they can't, we are going to have to rely on our brain, a clear brain Mooch. He pointed to his head. "This is the only thing that is going to aid us. Keeping it together and remaining cool. Okay. Are you all right?"

Mooch expelled a deep breath and whimpered. "I am so sorry for all this. This is all my fault, and I feel terrible cousin."

"Yes, Mooch, it is your fault and you should feel terrible. I couldn't agree with you more, but now is not the time to point fingers. It isn't going to help our situation."

Zeto shook his head and pulled on his whiskers, a habit he began in his youth and had tried to kick since adolescence. As much as he tired… when he got worked-up, he unconsciously stroked the white fur around his mouth and whiskers. Half the time he wasn't even aware that he was doing it.

With a serious expression plastered on his face, Zeto added in friendship, but also in warning. "The turbulence is about to begin and staying in control of yourself and using your head is our only hope. I have been trying to keep track of the direction he is taking us. Maybe we can use this information later. Remember what I said Mooch. Knowledge is our only hope and to keep our heads on straight."

Mooch smiled over at his cousin who had returned to his place across their small enclosure, feeling like he had been handed a golden egg presented on a golden platter and said, "I'll keep it together Zeto. I promise you I will keep it together. I'm not messing up anymore. I am going to use my head from this minute on, no matter what."

"That-a-boy. That's what I want to hear." Zeto replied as they passed a "**NO TRESPASSING**" sign and started down a one-lane gravel road. The vehicle crunched over the bumpy road and then came to a sudden stop.

Tucci's Mink farm supplied Milano's fashion industry with more than 20% of their mink products. To planet Earth and its human inhabitants, Milan reigned supremely as the primary center of world high fashion and was considered one of the leading business centers, as it remained the seat of the Italian Stock Exchange. Tucci's farm was not large or grand by any means, but providing that much mink had made him a comfortable living.

He stood in front of eight small Kit sheds he had built himself. He had larger, sturdier barrack-like structures for thousands of minks that stayed with him for longer periods of time. He liked to think of those structures as the family units. Those units contained minks that had never lived in the wild on their own. He raised most of them from little babies.

The smaller sheds, the eight he was looking at right now were for all his little furry friends that had lived outside on their own, in their natural habitat, the ones he trapped and captured and brought here.

There were eight red painted sheds and the newcomers always went to Shed #1. The minks in all of these sheds were used for his own personal use. It wasn't easy keeping that wife of his happy, so he did a little moonlighting on the side. He raised the cage, before unlocking the shed door and looked inside again at the mink with the unusual almost black pelt, appraising it quickly. He had never seen a coat this exquisite, this rare. It was sure to bring him a pretty penny. He placed their cage on the ground and fumbled with keys.

Well, little buddies, here is your new home." He picked the cage back up after unlocking the door and walked inside. Both

Mooch and Zeto tried to see their surroundings, but it was like someone had turned out the lights. They were taken from the dim brightness of an overcast winter morning into total darkness.

"Listen up all my little furry friends. You have new roommates so I expect you to be on your best behavior." He must have thought that was funny because he laughed. "I know we have both boys and girls in here so I repeat…no shenanigans."

His big red bulbous nose was almost pressed up against Mooch and Zeto's cage… "Newcomers, this is your new home."

He walked straight from the door into a narrow aisle just wide enough for him to make his way up and down between the cages. He placed their cage on a shelf that was comprised of two slats of wood with a strip of wire-mesh in the middle that ran along the entire length of the shed on both sides.

He looked into the cage and smiled. "At last, no more vacancies… I can now relax."

He started to leave, but turned as if forgetting something. "Oh yeah, I keep it mighty cold in here, got to keep that fur growing and thickening so that noise you hear above you is the overhead fan. Well, good day to you all. Make it a good one."

The shed was dark, but after his eyes adjusted, Zeto found that he could make a few things out. Enough light penetrated through the weathered slats, so the first thing that Zeto was able to identify, were that other cages were lined along this shelving in varying sizes and shapes. Some were square and some were rectangular, and each contained two to three minks. Calculating quickly as he glanced around, he estimated that between sixteen to maybe twenty some other minks occupied this shed. He wondered why the number was so small?

The second thing he noticed was the squalid smell and for a moment he used all his strength not to reach into his pocket for his, by now, used handkerchief. Then the murmuring began. He looked around at the rest of the minks as they whispered and stared, really at a loss for words.

Nothing in life had prepared him for this. His heart began to beat loudly. As he looked around, his eyes stopped in the third cage over and cattycorner from his, he noticed, could not help but to notice, one of the most beautiful female minks he had ever seen.

There were two females in the cage. One appeared to be very young and the other looked to be around his age so he didn't think the younger one could be her offspring. He caught himself and averted his eyes. Looking at a female while in the direst situation of his life? He pulled at his whiskers. Had he ever done anything like that before? What was wrong with him? *Was he finally losing his mind?*

"Excuse me," he spoke to them all and instantly the room was *drop-a-pin-on-the-floor-and-you-could-hear-it* quiet.

"I know who you are." A male mink in the cage directly across from him said. "You're that Count Aldofonso guy. Begging your royal pardon sire, but I have seen your picture many times. I am a subscriber to *Minks Monthly,* and *Ville & Casali,* so I have seen you featured many times. How in the heck did you get in here anyway, your royalness? Don't you have a small army of weasels or something protecting you all the time?"

"You are right. I am Count Zeto *Ul-de-ri-co*. I do have bodyguards, but they are minks just like you or me, not weasels. This is Muccino Alberdinni, but many refer to him as Mooch. Please tell why the…"

"How did Tucci get you guys?" the nameless mink cut him off mid-sentence. Zeto frowned. He could not remember a time when anyone would dare interrupt him. He was finding that this other half, the half that Mooch had wanted him to experience, lacked about every manner he could think of. Obviously these minks had never learned to revere others in higher stations. He narrowed his eyes, and turned toward Mooch.

Mooch raised his paw into the air and said, "That would be me. Unfortunately, I am the one who stupidly got us caught going after those stupid crayfish."

At hearing this, the entire room burst out into laughter. The same mink with no name said,

"That's how we all got here except for Adrianna. She got here trying to save her little niece Marcellina. But those darn crayfish did us all in…."

Zeto looked toward the direction the nameless one pointed. He could see her looking at him and as their eyes met, he felt his eyes go wide as something electric crackled through his body like a zap. This had to be stress? She lowered her eyes and stared down at the floor of her cage and Zeto turned back toward the mink that was still speaking, but he hadn't heard one single word he had said.

"Signore, I mean, hello there… sire, Count Ferico."

"Ulderico," he corrected curtly.

"Sorry, Count Ulderico."

"I'm sorry, and your name is?"

"Oh, everybody just calls me Frank. My full name is Francesco Giovanni DiRocco. Frank will be fine enough though."

"As I was saying…Signor Frank, please tell me everything you can about this place and maybe we can discover some means in which to free ourselves."

"With pleasure. Let me start out by introducing you to everybody in here. We are all on a first name basis, no formalities here, so I will make introductions that way.

My bunker here is Dominic." Dominic lifted his fore paw and waved. Dominic looked to be about Zeto's age.

"The cage over to my right here, we'll call it Cell #2, that's Arturo on your right, the middle one is Vincenzo and Plino is on the left." All three minks waved. Older, Zeto thought, maybe middle aged.

"In Cell #3, I already pointed out Adrianna and Marcellina." They both looked up, and again Zeto felt something strange, some foreign teeming current that he never experienced before.

"The fourth cage over would be Elda." Zeto looked at a

heavyset female mink. "Elda is a widow and that is her daughter Simona." They both waved and the little female minky giggled.

Frank dipped his head. "Sadly, her mate was here four years ago."

He cleared his throat and continued. "Now to your left, in Cell #5 are: Santo, Teodosio… but we all call him Teo, and Beppe with the mustache. Do not dare call him Giuseppe unless you want verbally pummeled." All three minks appeared older, in their twilight years.

"Next to them in Cell #6, are Renzo and Caterina, recently married and trapped while out on a moonlit honeymoon hunt." The both waved their paws and smiled. "Can you believe it? What lousy luck. Tucci got them while on their honeymoon? If that doesn't beat all."

"Last, but not least and in the seventh cage next to yours are our teenminkers: Castore, Venanzio and Fidele, all out carousing and getting into mischief somewhere I would presume." All three lifted their paws, as their names were being mentioned. One, Zeto thought was Venanzio yelled, "Hey, what up dude?"

"That's all of us. And now the two of you occupy the eighth cage--counting the two of you, nineteen in all. Within the last two weeks all of us have been taken from near our homes with the lure of those darn crayfish, irresistible to any mink."

Zeto looked around at a real mix of minks. Had they all shared their life stories? Become bosom buddies? Strangely, within the group, he sensed a friendly camaraderie; an unspoken fellowship among them for only having spent a short time together. It amazed him that they were all so calm and smiling and friendly with death staring them straight in the face. Did they not realize the imminent danger that they were all in? His stomach fluttered with a plopping sensation. Did they not understand where they were and what eventually would happen if they found no means of escape? It boggled his brain.

Everyone looked at him as though they expected him to say something. Did they expect him to break into his entire life history beginning with, *"a story about a young Italian Count?"* Did they expect him to come up with amusing ditties to entertain them while in confinement? He looked around at each of them and then he looked back at Frank.

"Tell me something Frank, why so few? From what I have picked-up over the years, these farms or ranches, whatever you want to refer to them as, hold sometimes up to 70,000 minks."

"They do." Frank replied. "The shed you are in has nineteen minks. We are all Tucci's trapped prizes. There are eight sheds that hold about twenty of us. That would make for about 160 minks. He has these massive structures on the other side of his farm with about 25,000 farm-raised minks. These are the minks that have never known freedom. That's where he makes his big money. I believe all of us are a little game to him. These sheds, from what he says, when he comes in and talks to us, are a hobby for him. He's a nut job, you know; -rabid… with the intelligence of a doorknob."

At this, the rest of the minks broke out into laughter.

"You heard him talking to us. Would you call *that* the ramblings of a sane mind? What we have gathered thus far, is that the humans have no hint about our world. None. When we talk we make sure we aren't understood. To him, we sound like chattering animals.

All this," Frank indicated the room, "isn't about human survival. We aren't harvested for food. We are harvested for the skin off our backs, as luxury items and he loves the rush, the hunt, and the challenge of outsmarting us. He does it for the sport… just for fun. Thank God he uses these traps and not Spring Traps or Leg Holds. Did you ever see an animal caught in one of those, the ones with steel teeth? Gives me the jitters just thinking about it"

"Why the number eight? Eight sheds?" Zeto asked.

Adrianna answered that question, her voice sultry; her speech -impeccable. "In eight months we will be euthanized. Each month he will move all of our cages to the next shed up, until we get to the last shed which is shed #8. That is his way of keeping track of the months we have been *boarding* with him. It seems Signor Tucci is too intellectually challenged to do it any other way."

Her niece, Marcellina shimmed under her fore arm and Adrianna held her close. "So in two weeks," she continued, "all of us will be moved up to shed #2 and so on and so forth. We are now his little *bambinos,* sometimes his little *buddies*. Depends on his mood. We are fed two meals a day, and kept in perpetually freezing temperatures so that our coats thicken more. Eight months seems to be about the norm with the facts and statistics I have read thus far."

And she *reads*! Zeto thought. A beautiful female with a brain. One that actually reads. Now that was something new to him.

Scrunched over, Zeto pulled at his whiskers. "Then we are going to have to pull our resources together and find a way out of here."

"Dude," Venanzio, the teenminker said, "like the three of us here have been working on this steel mesh for over a week and we have made some progress, but we have to keep it hidden so that old man Tucci doesn't find it. Castore here, he's small enough to squeeze through a small hole once we make it, and as soon as he's out, he can release all our cages... I think. Don't look too difficult man... just a few pins here and hook there and we're outta here like PRONTOOOO. It don't matter where he puts our cages, the wire underneath is aluminum and one bite of that and we've breached the old toilet screen."

"However," old mink Beppe interjected, "afterward, we have quite another problem."

"That being?" Zeto asked.

"The shed itself. We are locked in from the outside."

"I see. Suppose we release ourselves from these traps," Zeto said, "we would have to dig under these sheds and that would have to be done in the middle of the night to avoid detection and may take up to several days. Am I right?"

"Yes. When Tucci sleeps and several days." Bepe replied.

Zeto moved up to the trap door and tried to feel around. It would be impossible to release the door from the inside because the mesh was so fine and gathered that it would be impossible to get a paw through it, but from what he could see when he looked around at the other cage doors, he didn't think it should be too difficult a task. What he wouldn't give for a pair of sharp wire cutters.

Zeto studied the walls of the shed for a moment. "I believe these sheds are Kit sheds, made cheaply and from what I can see there is no foundation. Digging under it is our only hope."

He then turned to follow the perimeter, but it was difficult in so dark a place but he did notice an outline of white. He pointed to the floor. "Can someone please tell me what that white substance covering the perimeter of the floor is all about?"

"That is lime." Adrianna pointed around. "Lime is used to prevent the spreading of germs and disease."

Again, he had a hard time looking away. He could not believe her beauty or the song her voice seemed to sing. He wondered how long she and her niece had been in there.

"Then we can be easily tracked if walked upon. The dirt is pretty solid with the cold weather, I realize that, but that may be to our advantage--frozen earth leaves no tracks, but I am afraid it will be that much more difficult and take that much longer to tunnel under."

"Then that is our only way out." Beppe said. "We had pretty much concluded that."

"I don't know if this is any consolation, but I know that I am being scented as we speak. My family will not stop until I am found."

"How could they possibly help us?" Beppe asked. "I have a wife in shed #2 and I do not plan to leave here without her. We can't possibly dig under all these sheds without detection. It is hopeless."

Zeto considered that for a moment. "You minks have no idea what Signor Tucci will be facing if all my guards converge on this farm at once. They can and will destroy everything and anything in their path to prevent any harm from coming to me. We are talking about generations of well-trained ex-soldiers. I am sure my family will also bring in the highest level of Security. This level of Security is used primarily by the royal family, but because I am a *close relative,* my lineage spanning from King Orsini himself, I am positive my family would have brought them in."

Zeto blinked and looked around at all their blank faces. Expressionless eyes blinked back at him. "Is it something I said?" He looked over at Frank.

"Count," Frank began, "we are well aware that our sovereign and the Royal Armed Forces do not become involved in the human domain."

"I tell you my family will stop at nothing until I have been located and brought out of this place. They will figure a way to get me out without interfering in the world of the Homo Sapiens."

Zeto surveyed the others as he continued to speak. "What I

am telling you is true. They may have a problem with liberating all of us, but they will eventually come and they will destroy this shed!"

For the first time, everybody started to talk at once. Even Mooch who had remained miraculously quiet, was conversing with the their three adolescent mink neighbors next door.

Beppe made a shrilling scream and got everyone's attention. The room fell silent. "We cannot all talk at once. We will accomplish nothing. His voice had a new spring to it, a new lift

"Count Ulderico," he turned and faced Zeto with his snout pressed against his cage wall, "Sire, you have an army, not just any army, but an army of well-trained mink soldiers. All we have to do is get you out of here and you can bring them all back to destroy this death camp. That will expedite any plan that we can make for escaping. I think this is our one and only hope. Please, just hear me out, Count...

If we send more or if all of us leave, then Tucci will become suspicious and surely he will tighten his security, which will make it, that much more difficult for you and your minks to do what you know needs to be done. He will assume that humans against the farming of minks have liberated us, and will lay in wait. He and his crew will also stalk us relentlessly through the woods to recapture us. This I know. He has workers, hired help for the minks in the back. None that live on the premise, but nevertheless, men that can lay in wait and who can and will make it that much more difficult if not impossible for you and your soldiers to free us."

Zeto listened, but it took him a moment to comprehend

what was being suggested. "I don't know that I...."

"We could add a lot of fur into your cage," Beppe looked over at Mooch, ignoring Zeto, "and to Tucci, as dull as he is, it will seem like you, Signor Mooch had your bunkmate for breakfast one morning, bones and all...."

They all looked over at Mooch who began rubbing his big round belly right below his white spot, and winked at everyone. Their chuckles echoed off the tin roof. He too snorted with laughter, until all the laughter faded, and the room once again was plunged into a serious quietness.

Beppe jumped back in. "He is too thick-witted to come to any other conclusion."

He looked over at the teen minks. "Castore, Venanzio and Fidele will continue working on the wire until Castore can squeeze through it. They will have no trouble hiding their workmanship because they are working on the mesh on the bottom of their cage, then onto the wire strip between our timber-paneled shelves.

Castore will be able to slide down and out; although I am sure it will not be pleasant. I am sorry Castore," he turned to address the teen mink, "but as I told you before, like it or not, underneath, on the dirt floor lies nothing but raw filth. Hopefully for your sake, Tucci will have changed the hay by then, but you must remember not to touch any of the lime, or Tucci will notice your white tracks. But if it all works to plan then we can start the digging."

"Hey, I'm cool." Castore nodded. "My roomies here are

gonna have to put up with my stanky butt, it ain't like I can take a shower or nothing."

"You stink now," Fidele interjected. "You mean you're gonna smell worse?"

"Dudes, you *like* both reek." Venanzio pinched his nose.

Castore held his nose also and started to point. "Well you ain't exactly smelling like no petunia."

Beppe, with eyebrows furrowed, looked over at their cage. "Venanzio, Castore, Fidele...Enough.." All three immediately became still.

Frail old Beppe, white wisps of fur blew under the large industrial fan overhead as he looked back over at Zeto. "Count Ulderico." he said, slowly, careful to choose his words correctly. "You must be the one to go. You must be the one to follow the one road back to where you were trapped. At some point, I am hoping you can track your guards or they will be able to track you. There is no other way to hasten this matter."

Everyone's attention fell upon Zeto. He could feel perspiration form, his guts rolling into a solid tight ball. He sat there, every nerve standing exposed. His heart picked up pace as he watched all eyes focus on him. Mooch let his head drop down into his paws. The seconds ticked and the stretch of silence became uncomfortable, intolerable. Zeto pulled at his whiskers. Gingerly, he selected his words.

"Beppe is it?"

Beppe smiled and nodded.

"I think Signor Beppe that your idea is a good one, and it should be well executed but the fact is, that it is out of the question for me. I do not feel competent enough for this undertaking..."

"And why is this, Sire?"

"Let's just say that I think that Muccino may have a better chance at meeting success since he knows the terrain better than I. I am sorry, but I am just not familiar."

Mooch looked up from his paws, an expression of incredulity written all over his face. "*OH MAN*... Zeto please. There is no way."

"You can do this Mooch." Zeto looked into his eyes. "You would be better for this undertaking than I for reasons we are both aware."

"I... I c-c-can't," Mooch swallowed hard. "I can't. I'll flub it up. Come on Zeto, you know what I'm talking about. You can't seriously put all these minks' welfare in my hands. You're the one who thinks on his feet. The one who can talk yourself in and out of anything and take decisive action. Okay, so you don't see that well in the dark. Big deal. We all have our weaknesses. But you have that cool head. You've been raised with those skills since birth. You can think on your feet in extreme adverse situations. Please don't make me do this? I ... I. c-can't."

"Count Ulderico," he already knew her voice with its salty rich texture, "a problem with your vision? Please elaborate."

Zeto closed his eyes. His paws felt clammy. Then he turned to face her. "I have no night vision. I am totally blind in the dark."

The shed stilled. No one spoke. He could feel their questioning eyes on him. And still no one spoke.

"Is it possible to make this trip in daylight?" Adrianna asked. *At last someone spoke.* "How far were you and Signor Mooch away from your ancestral seat when you were trapped?"

Zeto turned to Mooch.

Mooch looked back thinking and finally said, "From where we were picked up, maybe four kilometers? Give or take a few meters here or there. But it is a tricky four kilometers. There are lots of twists and turns and lots of back woods to contend with. When he nabbed us...." Mooch tried to avoid using the word *trapped.*

"I would say that we were about four, but I can't be sure, but from there, we were thrown in the back of his motorized vehicle and driven away. I could never figure distances from moving human vehicles. In school I was terrible in math... remember those word problems when they expected us to figure out..."

"Just answer the question." Zeto snapped impatiently.

"Let me think here for a minute. I'dle know. If I had to guess, I would say that we were in the back of that thing for about twenty minutes maybe more. The road was really bumpy I remember that, and he was driving slowly.

"Would you say he was moving at fifteen to twenty kilometers per hour?" Adrianna asked.

"Like I said Signora or is it Signorina?

96

"Signorina." Her head tilted to the side.

"It could have been. As I said, up to this point in my life, I have never been in a moving contraption like that before. We were moving at a pretty slow clip; the road we were on was narrow with lots of sharp bumps, bends and curves like I said. We had to clutch the bottom so we wouldn't be thrashed around inside."

Adrianna remained quiet for several moments. "Let me try to figure this out using the maximum of numbers with the information you have given me thus far. I would rather overestimate than underestimate it. If you were on the road, for twenty minutes, going approximately twenty kilometers per hour," she said thinking out loud, "then he probably drove... let me think this out for a minute.

Rate times the time is equal to the distance. So if your time was twenty minutes and you were traveling at approximately twenty kilometers per hour, then a close estimation on how far you traveled by truck, by the way, that moving contraption you were referring to, is called a *pick-up truck*, you would be about six kilometers away. That could take a day; more likely two and that would be pushing it even traveling at a fast pace. Two days of almost constant travel."

She gazed back over at Zeto, whom she noticed was already staring back at her. *He could not see at night? That was unheard of. She had never met a mink in her life with this particular type of night disability.*

"Your night blindness, Count Ulderico, a born birth-defect, or something you developed over a period of time?"

"It is not a birth defect and I did not develop it over a period of time. There is nothing physically or functionally wrong with my eyes." He could feel his cheeks burning, his voice resentful. What did she think he was? Did she think he was some sort of little *weakling*?

"I don't understand."

"No one's asking you to understand," he said sharply, but found himself explaining. "I never had to depend upon night vision for anything therefore, it was never developed. Maybe there is something to *not using and losing*?"

"You never used your night vision?" He could hear bewilderment in her voice.

He cleared his throat and started to shake his head back and forth and circle the white fur around his mouth with his left paw. "No. I have never used my night vision."

A hush fell over the group.

He looked down and cleared his throat again. "As I said, I never needed to."

"Then how do you hunt?" Adrianna asked, her eyes full of wonderment.

Zeto pulled at his whiskers as he glared at her indignantly, unmistakable outrage in his voice. "Can we please change this subject and drop the inquiry. I feel like I'm standing in front of the Spanish Inquisition. Listen, I just got here. I am on a fact-finding mission. I don't know how my personal life and habits are relevant here."

"I don't believe Sir," her voice had an edge, "that my inquiry was of any specific interest in your personal life or habits. I have never met an adult mink that did not use their night vision to hunt. I was naturally curious, that is all." At that she turned her back to him and walked to the corner of her cage and sat down.

No one would dare use that tone on him now, Zeto thought. Who did she think she was anyway? What was wrong with all these minks? Didn't they understand who he was?

"Dude, like same question," Venanzio interjected excitedly, "Sorry man, but I gotta ask. How do you eat, like, do you pay somebody to go out and do all your hunting for you? Like that would be kinda cool I guess. But I kinda like it, although it can be a pain in the butt sometimes...."

Zeto closed his eyes and took a deep breath. He was certain that this was the very first time in his life that he felt embarrassed by his lifestyle. And why? What did any of them know? They didn't know him. Let them think what they wanted. Why should he care?

"I have always had my food prepared for me." Simple enough answer, so why was he sounding so defensive? He didn't know why he felt he owed anyone an explanation. It was of no concern to any of them, so why was he still explaining? "I never learned or felt the need to acquire this ability.

Very few minks in my family, for generations needed their night vision as a means of survival, and stop me if I am wrong, but I fail to see how any of this matters or pertains to the situation at hand." Yet, for some ridiculous reason, it did matter.

He glanced back over at *her,* and her back was still toward him. Why should he care what she thought of him--he didn't even know her? He never gave any female's first impression of him a second thought. He would have to think about this later when he was no longer on center stage, and then he could really analyze the dynamics going on here.

The murmuring began instantly. *Boy, this day had come full-circle,* Zeto thought.

"Then you can learn to get it all back." It was Beppe who spoke again. "It takes 75 adult minks to make one full length mink coat. Did you know that? Were you aware of that? On the other side of this farm, there are long wooden structures that are covered with tin roofing where upon entering you will see columns and rows of stacked shelving so long in fact, that Farmer Tucci has to sit on a riding motorized vehicle to feed all the minks in there. There is not one, but two of these structures, housing near to 25,000.

Thousands trapped in tiny little rectangular boxes. Compared to them, our accommodations are like suites at the Four Minkson's. We need to be liberated. *All of us.* And you have to be the one to do it. We will worry about the others once we are freed. Maybe there is something your soldiers could do for them also."

Zeto began to shake his head.

Bepe looked over at his cage. "Just wait and listen to what I have to say, please. I have lived a long time and I have watched our kind disappear, our numbers are slowly dwindling. No one lifts a finger, no one gets involved because we think…that'll never happen to me…and guess what? We wake up one day in a cage. Our live expectancy is suddenly a lot shorter. If someone were to free all those minks that never had the opportunity to run free, hunt for themselves, see in the night to hunt for themselves, yes, many would not survive, many would die, I realize that, but staying put and doing nothing, ***all of them will die.*** There will be *no* chances for them. At least if they are freed, their odds increase by fifty-fifty."

Adrianna had stood up and turned and was listening to what Beppe, was saying, then added, "The mink farmers would like everyone to believe the propaganda that the farm-raised will perish from starvation or predators because they have never had to fend for themselves, but there is no literature, no studies, no concrete conclusive evidence to support this. Nothing from what I have come across thus far in my reading proves these conjectures.

There are many agricultural scientists and groups that have studied this phenomenon and how it affects the ecosystem and they concur that many of these farm-raised minks can live and survive in the wild, especially in areas where food is abundant, ~plentiful. Many make it because their natural abilities kick in. It is like they shift into automatic pilot."

"Yes, my dear Adrianna," Beppe said excitedly. "And said so eloquently. This is exactly what I was getting to…."

Frank looked over at Beppe. "So what are you suggesting?"

"I believe that once our Count is free, all his natural abilities, as Adrianna so poignantly put it, will snap back into place. Of course, this isn't going to happen over night. Time is on our side. We are in the first shed." He looked over at Zeto with pleading eyes. "We can help you as much as we can."

"Is anyone listening to me?" Zeto's voice became formal, fierce. "I will not accept the responsibility to liberate this entire mink farm. I do not have that kind of power that would be necessary in order to free this entire mink population. Do not depend on me. If you depend on me, then *you are all fools*! None of us will make it out! Capisci?"

He looked around at all their faces while a lengthy silence followed. His eyes met Adrianna's. They were beautiful eyes. Brown with tiny flecks of gold, and thick long black lashes he could see from here. His body stiffened. How could he see her eyes and lashes in here? Granted he could see from the little bit of light that peaked through the slats, but it *was* pretty dark because no sun shone through. It was a cold dreary typical winter day.

The silence continued to grow. He moved to the back corner of his cage feeling more trapped than he did at the moment the door of this prison cell clicked shut. And still the silence. He closed his eyes and rested his head back against unyielding mesh. Did they not understand the gravity of what they were asking him to do? Did it not sink in that there would be no happy endings with him at the helm?

He knew that his guards and the specialists his mother probably brought in were well trained enough to pick up his scent and would bypass any other mink and that the process would move faster if he were to go, and that was assuming they could dig under and escape.   He was sure that he had been tracked to where they had been taken prisoners, but from there the trail, his scent, would have grown cold by now.

Six or more kilometers of back woods that ran perpendicular to a one-lane road alone? No. It was not possible. The notion, absolutely ridiculous… laughable in fact.

How ironic, he thought, that the last relative he had spoken about on his last day of freedom had been his great, great, Great-Uncle Salvatore who ended up wrapped around Queen Victoria's neck so many years ago. He married a commoner, had been disowned by his family which meant no more guard privileges, and a mink stole he became… and all for love.

Zeto sighed and twisted his neck around and rubbed his eyes. How had he become this tired when so much adrenalin had been flowing only moments earlier? Right now all he wanted to do was sleep….

Chapter Five

Adrianna

Contessa Arabella sat across from her brother picking at her food. How could she eat? The thought of food turned her stomach. She looked over at her brother, her dear sweet Angelo who had never failed her, and watched as he finished his meal. He looked up at her and his eyes softened.

"Bella," He had called her Bella since she was a minky, *beautiful one*, as did her late husband, Salvo. Her husband was so like her brother, it was no wonder she had loved him so.

"You have got to eat little sister. You need to keep up your strength."

"Oh, Angelo, sweets," she leaned forward and reached out and covered her paw over his, "thank you for coming. I couldn't bear this alone. Two days Angelo, two whole days and each day his scent evaporates a little more and a little more. Soon there will be no scent at all. There will be nothing. Then my life will be over."

"Dear sister of mine," he lifted her chin in his paw and examined her face. He moved it slowly to the left and then to the right. She was still a beautiful mink, but a sad and tired looking one. "You speak of him as though he is never to return. I think that what they discovered is very positive. We know he was scented to that crab place and then to that other place, the one they said was a literal hole in the ground. What kind of place is called *Road Kill* and better yet, why Zeto would ever be within 500 paces of either one of those two places remains a mystery to me, but it reeks of Muccino.

They do not sound like places *our* Zeto would step a paw into. Muccino's scent gland was picked up not far from that Road place. I gather that something extremely intense happened, but the very positive side of that is that our minks would have picked up some scent of a struggle or a kill, and that was *definitely* not scented. Many of the minks that were present the night Zeto and Muccino were there, are being interviewed as we speak. We'll know more shortly when the team of specialists are brought in. I have also sent for all my minks. They should be here within the hour."

"When are these specialists coming? How much longer do we have to wait? My son is out there somewhere, lost... maybe injured, and possibly... I can't even speak the word."

Her eyes pleaded. "Why is the Grand General taking his good old sweet time bringing them here? Why can't he hurry? Can't you expedite this some way Angelo? Can't they see that if Zeto *could* come home, that he would? Can't they see that he might be held against his will somewhere? My heart Angelo," she placed her paw over her heart, "is breaking Angelo, it's breaking!"

"Bella, calm down." He took her paw and began to stroke it. He watched big tears begin their descent down her cheeks. "These matters take time," he countered. "They are sending in the very best and when you are dealing with the best, waiting is always involved. These minks are soldiers, trained so well, that they will know exactly what happened, when it happened and where it happened by scenting alone. A little snow means *nothing* to them.

As hard as I know it is, please try to be patient. I am sure the Grand General is doing the very best he can. We are lucky to have relatives in such high places to do such favors for us."

Contessa Arabella swiped at her wet cheeks. Her husband's family was among the highest in the royal family. He was a descendant of a king. "Zeto where are you?" She repeated the same litany hourly. "Please try and find your way back home."

"We'll find him." Angelo sighed deeply. His fur had grayed. She had not noticed that before. "We will find him and when we do, I am going to turn him over my knee and give him a good thrashing for scaring us so badly. I don't care how old he is. I love him too, Bella. He is my heir and the son I never had. Things have a way of working out. You'll see. I just don't understand something. Maybe you can clear it up for me. Muccino Alberdini, wasn't his father the one that absconded with all that money in the Royal Treasury he had been entrusted with, never to be seen or heard from again?"

The Contessa sighed. "His mother raised him alone, facing a titan of scorn her husband branded them with. He abandoned them both for money. Muccino maybe a little wild; rough around the edges, but he has had to hurtle incredible odds just to walk with his head up."

Angelo shook his head. "Why Zeto tolerates him is a mystery to me."

"Because my son has a good heart, so much like you Angelo, and don't forget, Muccino *is* related. He is Zeto's third cousin on his father's side."

"Third cousins are like no relative at all, and I have a funny feeling Muccino is behind all of this mayhem. The Zeto I know would never walk through those front doors," he pointed, "let alone at night, without proper security, and then to go to those two awful places unless Muccino was behind it someway, somehow. I tell you, I smell Muccino in all of this. I told you to discourage that friendship years ago."

"Muccino makes Zeto laugh. And he is rather sweet once you get to know him. Zeto tell us there is more to Muccino than meets the eye, and he should know. They went away to school together. Their friendship goes way back. Salvo and I found nothing wrong with their friendship as far back as I can remember. I think in many ways Zeto feels sorry for him. He is a grown mink, making grown adult mink decisions, carrying on with all of Salvo's duties and responsibilities, and if he likes having Muccino around, then that is his prerogative. Let's not discuss Muccino. I just want my son back."

She stood from the table and slowly made her way over to large Palladian windows that stood on either side of a granite fireplace and looked out. *Where are you my son?* She leaned her head against a frosted pane. *Where are you?*

***

Giuseppe Tucci relished his job and did it with a smile on

his face and a lift in his heels. He took great pride in his work that he did and an appreciation for all his furry friends that made it all possible. Frozen snow crunched under foot as he made his way to the first shed and unlocked the door.

"Din-din time," he yelled as he opened the door. He clicked on an overhead light and his furry buddies came to life, and began their chatter. He sat an industrial five-gallon bucket on the floor of the shed and bent down to scoop food from it.

"What do we have in here? Oh wow! Ground raaaabbitttt! Boy-o-boy you minks are sure lucky to have such a mouth-watering dinner prepared for you. ...If only my wife cooked this good."

He stuck a scoop of cold ground rabbit into a portable tray and pushed it back into their cage. "Hellooooo neeeeeeeewcomers."

His face was almost pressed against the mesh. "I grind all your food up for you. Don't want any of you to choke. See what a nice guy I am? So... yummy... yummy... yummy in your tummy... tum... tummy!"

...Up to this point, Zeto had never been a violent mink. He had been brought up to use diplomacy in sticky situations. He had never been in a physical altercation in his entire life, but this brainless bozo was starting to push his buttons and he had almost reached the red one right in the middle. He wanted to jump through the steel wire and claw at his face, especially that smug smile he wore. He watched him as he half sang, half talked to each occupant and then he turned around and said, "Good night my little buddies.

Make it a good one."

Zeto looked over at Mooch and then down at the metal tray that had been pushed through. He watched Mooch dip his claw into it and bring it to his mouth. "What exactly is that disgusting heap... oh, forget it. I don't want to know."

"Not bad. Really." Mooch dipped his head into it and started to chow.

"You never could pass up a meal could you?"

"Ouch. Now that wasn't a very nice thing to say," Mooch replied with his mouth full. "I happen to be hungry."

"Yeah... well it's your hunger that got us into this mess in the first place. And could you please chew with your mouth shut. For years now I have been tolerating that open-mouthed chewing thing you do, but in truth, it really repulses me."

Mooch closed his mouth immediately and finished chewing, but there was very little to chew since it had already been ground for them.

"I'm sorry Zeto." Mooch said with conviction. "You have every right to be mad at me. I got us into this mess. I can't tell you how sorry I really am. But I think you need to eat some of this because you haven't had anything to eat since Crabby's and when you think about it that was almost two days ago."

"Mooch, believe it or not, we are not all professional eaters... controlled by our stomachs. We do not all live to eat. Some of us actually eat to live, and right now the only way I would ever eat that garbage is if you handed me a large pair of wire cutters so I could cut my way out of this filthy hovel. And we both *know* what the odds are of that happening...."

"It really isn't bad, cousin, really it isn't." Mooch tried to placate, watching Zeto's expression bounce between disgust and fury. "Think of it as eating a cold rabbit leg from the frig."

"I do not eat cold rabbit legs from the frig. I do not eat rabbit legs, let alone eat them cold."

Mooch continued to nibble, but he concentrated on keeping his mouth shut while he did it.

Zeto felt like ripping his fur out. He was no longer afraid. Now he was mad. Furious. He hated this feeling of helplessness, of being powerless. He sat in a position of power his entire life only to end up like this? Maybe he would feel better if he could see something. Maybe he would feel better if he could actually smell something. The shed had grown darker and he looked around at them all eating the slop they had been given as though it were a seven-course meal served at a five star restaurant. It made him sick just watching them.

He walked to the corner of his cage, sat down and tried to get comfortable, but it was of no use. These cages weren't built for comfort. He couldn't stand-up. He couldn't stretch. The cage was low, so he had to move around it in a perpetual squat, and when he tried to lie down, wire mesh dug through his fur into his flesh. He could feel his blood boiling. The idea! This was an outrage! What was wrong with these minks?

From what he could see, they were hunched over eating like cud-chewing cows. The shed had grown even darker, and yet, he could make out cages and the minks in them. No fine detail, but he could distinctly see their outlines and movement, the way they bent or turned, as he watched them eat.

He glanced around the room. His eyes fell on Adrianna watching her niece as she ate. He wondered why she wasn't eating? As if sensing him, she turned her head and looked straight at Zeto, and again that stupid heart thing began. He knew what was wrong with him. He needed to get out of this place and he needed to get out of here now!

"It will get better for you," he heard her say, "if that is any consolation. At first, it is the most horrific feeling in the world. I would never wish this on my worst enemy."

"For some reason, Signorina Adrianna, I find it difficult to believe that you could ever have an enemy."

"Oh, you would be surprised," she had a soft soothing voice. "When we were first brought here eight days ago, I thought I would lose my mind. I felt like I was literally jumping out of my skin. My brain kept screaming that this wasn't really happening. I was losing myself in tidal wave upon tidal wave of panic. Of course I knew I couldn't. I have her," she nodded toward Marcellina, "so I had to keep it together. She is my brother's eldest daughter."

Marcellina looked up and smiled a wide grin. "Aunty A, please eat something. It's not that good, but you hardly ate anything all week."

Adrianna turned toward her niece and said, "Let's not worry about me. I am fine. Go ahead. If I want any, I will let you know."

Adrianna turned back toward Zeto. He could almost see her blink through what was left of the light. "It will get better Count. The others, all of us try to keep talking and somehow the time moves faster. If we didn't have each other, we would have lost our minds by now."

"If you don't mind me asking a personal question," Zeto said, "what is your profession?"

"Now there's a question almost too personal to answer." She had an amused jingle in her voice. And he felt himself smile. "I am a teacher. An instructor at University."

"In Rome?" he asked.

"The one."

"Well that's impressive." He walked passed Mooch who was still gobbling and stood at the end of the cage, the edge closest to her.

"And what does one instruct there?"

"Classical and Hellenic Studies mostly. I just received a full professorship, but am probably fired by now for not reporting to work or calling in sick."

"When we get out of here, they will understand and accept you back."

"When." She smiled, but knew he couldn't see it. "I like that."

A silence covered the shed. Only gusts of whipping wind moaning outside penetrated the shed. The others, he knew, sat listening.

"In the morning he will come back in and take us outside for fresh air. Signor Tucci believes that mink fur needs frigid fresh air. We see daylight Monday through Friday.

"You have picked up much in only a week." He heard himself make a sound, not quite a chuckle?

"When there is nothing else to do but sit here, it is amazing what one picks up. The hour grows late. It was nice conversing with you Count Ulderico."

"Zeto. Please."

"Okay then," her voice purred in his ears. "Goodnight Zeto."

Zeto could see Mooch watching him like a lovesick cow. He felt tiny pinpricks of guilt at the way he had spoken to him, not that he didn't deserve every word. He knew several others were not asleep, he could hear murmurs from the newlyweds, Renzo, was it, and his wife Caterina?

He curled himself into a ball, trying to find a comfortable position and closed his eyes. But now he found himself not sleepy. His mind was shooting all over the place. He wondered if he would live long enough to have a wife and little minkies? He thought of Adrianna. So smart. So beautiful. So young. So accomplished. He *had* to come up with something. He uncoiled himself and looked over at the cage next to him. He could see one of the three amigos sitting in the corner nearest him.

"Venanzio," he whispered. "Are you awake?"

"Dude, like how can anybody sleep in these miserable boxes?"

"I know. It's miserable." It was hard to believe that Venanzio was not much younger than he.

"Yeah, well try it with three to a box. There's just the two of you. There's no room to even breathe in here, not that you would want to anyway man, because these other two are like really ranking."

"How much progress have you three made on the mesh?" Zeto asked.

"This stuff is pure steel mesh man. It's the heavy-duty top of the line stuff. Like dude, false teeth for me if we ever get outta here cause there ain't gonna be any teeth left when we're finished with this."

"Just keep at it. That is the biggest and most important task. How much progress have you three made?"

"We got this small hole started. I'd say, we like, chewed about five connecting wires out. We're trying to be careful not to cut our gums. That's all we need, and then it'll be like infection city... can't risk it man."

"Five connecting wires? Just keep going. You guys are doing a great job." Zeto added, "and are our only hope. Only Castore is small enough to squeeze through a hole too small to be detected."

"Like, Dude… we are doing the best we can. I want outta here as much as anyone. I got a life too. I got a real babe waiting. She's like on fire, man, like smokin' … I got so-so parents and three pains in the butt sisters. We'll get it done. We got no choice."

"Get some sleep if you can," said Zeto. "You need your rest for more chewing and clawing tomorrow."

"Yeah. I guess you're right. Goodnight Count. And by the way, my friends call me Ven."

"Well then… Goodnight Ven…."

…Zeto sat hunched over and looked around at complete blackness, no light penetrated from anywhere, but he could still make-out the outline of cages and those in them. Something was happening. In the last two nights, changes were occurring that had him baffled. Something inside him was shifting, changing and he did not know why or if it would continue.

His sight showed marked improvement. He could see more than mere shadows and outlines even in the blackest part of nightfall. He had never endured long stretches of time spent in the darkness as he did right now. His world had been all about brightness, clear skies, and sunshine. He had basically lived in perpetual daylight. But he could feel this shift, something at work, progression inside him and he decided that he would accept whatever the possibility. It made him think of something he had read about in passing once, *Scotopic Adaptation*, also known as *dark adaptation.*

With these prolonged periods of darkness, maybe this was what was happening to him. His pupils were dilating which would increase the number of rods and decrease the number of cones, allowing him sharper sight in the dark. That made sense.

He was going to try as hard as he could to develop whatever abilities he had been born with. If he got out of here, he promised himself that he would do more things for himself so he would never be in a position in his live again to be so dependent on others. He would hone whatever skills he got back, if he got anything back. But no matter what, he promised himself that he would never feel this handicapped again. If the entire place blew up tomorrow, he would still be dependent upon others to see for him and scent for him and even hear for him.

He looked over to the third cage. He could see Adrianna's outline, even that her tail was wrapped around her niece. He smiled. He could also add *protector* to her list of attributes.

He couldn't remember meeting any female like her, and something told him that he never would again. He pulled at his whiskers. He would have to think about all this.

***

"Rise and shine my little sleepy heads." Farmer Tucci yelled as the door of the shed banged open. Dim light stung Zeto's eyes as he started to wake. What the heck time was it anyway? The crack of dawn?

"Minks in Shed #1 hear this--hear this. This is your central broadcasting system. This is a test, only a test. For the next three hours your cages will be sitting outside in the cold so that your fur will grow thicker for me."

He tried to make his voice sound like a public announcement over a loud speaker and laughed, "Come on, shake them lazy bones honeychile. We gonna have us a picnic outing down by the seashore.... Grab a few towels and some suntan lotion."

Tucci cracked up and started to grab the handles on the top of each of the cages. "You know Shed #1 always gets the sunshine first. Gotta get that early morning fresh air. Monday through Friday, thems the rules. Come on my little bambinos…"

He started lugging their cages out of the shed into the freezing predawn light. There was hardly a contrast between the freezing temperatures outside and the shed's interior. Zeto held on as he and Mooch were carried outside and practically thrown on the ground. He sat upon frozen snow. When did it start snowing he wondered? A nervous voice in his head told him that snow would not help his cause. Snow buried scents.

Adrianna and Marcellina's cage was placed smack up against theirs, and on the other side sat Edna and her groggy daughter Simona, followed by Santo, Teo, and Beppe, and next to them Renzo and his wife Caterina. The cages across, that butted up against there's was Arturo, Enzo and Plino, followed down the line by Castore, Venanzio, and Fidele, and finally Dominic and Frank.

All cages touched the next, until he had all eight cages placed smack together in an almost perfect rectangle.

"I'll be back in three hours with your grits. Enjoy the morning air my little bambinos. Make it a good one." And on that note, he turned and walked off toward the next shed.

Zeto looked over at Adrianna wrapping her niece into her heavy, extremely attractive tail.

"That man is a menace to society," she seethed as she cuddled closer with her niece. "Go back to sleep Marcellina, we're okay. He just brought us outside again. Go back to sleep sweetheart."

Zeto tried to go back to sleep as many of the others did since they had all been up practically half the night. He curled himself in the corner, crossed his fore arms in front of himself to shelter himself from the cold, and said, "If anyone thought that minks do not ever get cold, has another thing coming to them. It is freezing out here! I would like to stick that oversized lard-brained lunatic into a small uncomfortable enclosure and leave him out in the snow for three hours and see how he likes it. What I wouldn't do. What I wouldn't give."

"Now be nice Count Ulderico," Adrianna whispered looking over at him, "we have small ears listening."

"Zeto. I thought we corrected the name thing two nights ago." She smiled at him with a smile that could light any room and his heart began another round of heavy thumping. He wondered if she could hear it? He stood and practically crawled over to the

119

corner of the cage nearest her. He had never been this close to her before or in actual light, well an almost actual light and his breath caught in his throat as he became aware that she was even more beautiful than what he initially thought.

Count Zeto Pantaleone Ulderico whom had never been at a loss for words could not speak, became suddenly brain dead, a flat liner. The only body organ that seemed to be functioning at the moment was his heart. Bursting and booming away... *thud... thud... thud.*

Her fur was the deepest of brown, but with ash highlights as though the tips were dipped in honey, lighter eyes, more amber flecks than he had originally thought, golden light looked out at him from between long thick black lashes. Her ears were small and he noticed that she had flawlessly manicured claws. Her lips were full and looked soft, and her scent, a powerful sweetness that almost knocked him over. Scent? *He could smell her?* How could he smell her? He had never scented another female mink in is life. Is that what he was doing? Was he scenting her?

"Zeto, are you alright?" He felt himself shaken from his trance. He hadn't taken his eyes off her, and he was so close that he could almost reach out and touched her.

"Yes. I'm fine." Zeto cleared his throat. "I was just thinking about all the places I would like to see Farmer Tucci stuffed, but I guess I will keep that to myself since we have small, possibly awake ears listening."

"I was worried about you there for a minute."

Zeto remained mute. *What the heck was going on here? What was wrong with him?* He shook his head. It was this confinement. Locked in steel wire. Had to be. He wasn't himself. His nerves were raw, edgy. He tried to think of something to say, but all he could do was *smell* her sweetness, a fragrance so appealing that he could not seem to formulate a sentence. His tongue felt thick. He shook his head again and pulled at the dark whiskers around his mouth. *SAY SOMETHING YOU IMBECILLE!* Zeto summoned his vocal chords to do something.

"Sooooooo… Signorina Adrianna," he heard himself finally say, "how is it that you know so much about mink ranches? My first morning here you were spouting off statistics that would have impressed an adult human rancher."

"I majored in Agricultural Engineering before I changed over to Hellenic Literature. I decided I would rather venture into the past, studying classical mythology and live in a fabled world than deal with the real one. The Greek culture and its history, true or lure has always fascinated me. And you Count, I mean Zeto, what is your profession, besides being a Count?"

Zeto considered this question for a second or two and decided to answer it honestly. "I go to lots of parties. I eat lunches with state diplomats. I sit on various boards and committees so numerous I can't count. I track business ventures. I exercise five times a week to stay in shape. I listen to opera and have traced my genealogy several times over. Oh, and I am a collector of rare vintage wines which I keep well stocked in a custom-made wine cellar. How is that for starts? Impressed?"

Adrianna's eyes twinkled as he spoke. "Well, at least you're honest. Let me rephrase the question. What would you *like* to do had you not been born a Count?"

"You know, that is a very good question." Zeto had to think. "One that has never been posed to me before. ...I guess I would probably do what I studied in school; a subject that has always been of great interest to me, and that would be to continue in some capacity in the field of Mink Sociology, or European Mink Evolution. I actually studied, under Savino Tosana and Enrico Constanti, both tops in their field."

"Now *I* am the one to be impressed. That's an impressive duo." She watched a smile bloom on his face and she melted. Not only gorgeous, but there may be a sweet side. Maybe he wasn't totally sour after all. In truth, these last couple of days, she was finding him very easy to talk to. She thought she might rescind her initial impression.

"And why have you not continued in this field that interests you?"

"Boy, you are full of interesting questions. I have never considered that."

"I'm sorry. I didn't mean to pry," she said quickly. "That is a bad habit of mine. Asking questions and prying. Too naturally curious for my own good"

"You can ask me anything." Zeto said emphatically,

looking into her eyes and smiling that crooked smile that had her heart racing. "But really. Truly. Honestly. I never had any inking to actually work in a profession until I was locked up in here. Now I can think of a hundred different professions that have at one point been of some interest to me. It's funny what being incarcerated can make one think about. Not one mink in my family has ever *worked,* and so, I never tossed it around much. Then my father passed away two years ago, about the time I was finishing my studies and I took over as I was born to do. Very little of my time is really my own. There is always some place I have to be, some event I have to chair, some speech for some particular charity I have to give. Time owns me. It truly rules over me body and soul."

She blinked her eyes and thought about that for a minute. "But what about Zeto, the mink. What does *he* want?"

You, he thought. "I have not had a lot of time to think about any of that, but again, this abduction and incarceration is giving me a great deal of time to do just that. And what about you? Let me turn that question around? What is it that Adrianna wants?"

Her laughter warmed him. Literally. He was no longer freezing. "I am sorry for laughing, but my answer is so different from yours. I am doing *exactly* what I have always wanted to do, what I have always intended on doing. I love to teach. Developing and shaping the minds of our youth is so rewarding to me. So few of us get to do what we actually love, and I am lucky enough to be doing just that. I wouldn't trade it for all the muskrat pie in Europe."

"How do you do it?" He asked.

"Do what?" she answered.

"Live with all that passion." His voice was suddenly serious. "I wish I could feel a fraction of it. The way you talk... The overwhelming sense of joy of being so totally enthralled in what you do; the zeal of exciting others. I bet you are an excellent teacher."

Instinctually, Adrianna placed the palm of her paw against the cold mesh. "You will find your niche one day, and when you do, your passion will come. She pointed at his chest. "It's in here. ...*Your kingdom of dreams*... That's where you'll find it."

He looked up at her, and did something totally uncharacteristic; he placed his open palm against the freezing mesh. "My kingdom of dreams," he said feeling warmth from her paw. "You know, I don't even know your last name?"

"Benini. Originally from Tuscany." She said as she lowered her paw.

"Adrianna Benini from Tuscany, I want to know everything about you."

"Count Ulderico, there is really nothing to tell. My life is really too ordinary to recount."

"Then humor me, and don't leave anything out. Anything."

"Well, as I said, I was born in Tuscany, but my family moved to Rome when my father accepted a full professorship as head of the Mathematics Department at Rossi University in Rome. I have one brother, Marcellina's father, Leonardo. My father was a brilliant mink."

"Was?" Zeto asked.

"Was. He died when I was still young." She smiled up at him, but he could see tears forming in her eyes.

"I don't want you to talk about this if it upsets you."

"It upsets me, but I want to talk about it. Really. I love to talk about my father. You see, he was so very brilliant, such a life force, and in the prime of his life, teaching university level *Linear Algebra, Analytical Geometry*, something like *Calculus V*, when he was taken from us." She bent her head and leaned forward and whispered so softly. "He stepped into a mink trap and we never saw him again. He could have been at this very farm. Now wouldn't that be irony?"

Zeto was stunned for a moment. Had he become so callous, that he had become oblivious to the unfortunate minks he had read about ending up in places like this? Never to see a father or a sister or your child? Did he think himself exempt? Because it happened so rarely in the circles he traveled, was he convinced that it could never happen to him? When had he become so apathetic? When did he stop feeling? When had disdain for the common mink creep into his life? What had happened to him? He bent down on his haunches, below her bent head and looked up at her. "We are going to get out of here Adrianna. This I promise." He could see a tear spill over and slowly cascade down her face. "Believe me?"

She shook her head *yes*, wiping her eyes. Embarrassed. "I

125

don't know what got into me. I am sorry." She started to smile,

Still looking up, Zeto said, "Please don't be sorry. I feel honored that you shared that with me."

"I haven't cried once since that trap door came down enclosing us. I don't usually cry like this, especially to strangers."

"I am no longer a stranger." Zeto stood back up. "I would like to think that we are friends. Andrianna smiled over at him.

"I have never met anyone quite like you in my life." He leaned in so that his face was pressed against their barrier and whispered, "And I don't think I ever will. Now I can also add "brave" to your list of attributes."

"You have a list?" She grinned.

"Oh, I have a list. A very long list." He couldn't understand this boldness, so unlike him, but something felt right. She felt right. "So how did you come to be enclosed in your cage?"

"Marcellina and I often went on what we called *nature hunts*. Not only did we hunt, we also stopped and talked about various trees and their leaves and bushes, lakes, streams, et cetera, and I turned just as she was moving toward the trap; I could smell the crayfish before I actually saw her moving toward it. And something just clicked. I knew. I yelled, and grabbed for her, but it was too late. The door made a faint *click*. And here we are. …And you? Muccino mentioned that he caused your predicament."

Zeto looked over at Mooch. He still slept or pretended to sleep, it was hard to tell. "I can't put all the blame at his feet. Had I had my night vision, I think I could have done something to prevent

126

this. I didn't even smell the crayfish until we were practically sitting on it."

"It is very difficult to spot a trap at night anyway. In daylight they are a little easier. Leaves and twigs practically plastered all over them, --the bottom, top and sides, and of course the bait at the far end. And you know there are several different kinds of traps. I am just thankful we didn't meet a trap that springs out of nowhere and holds the prey with steel teeth. The mink either starves to death, becomes prey to another animal, or expires from injury.

...Even I, night vision and all, would have had a hard time spotting any kind of trap at night."

"How did you get so knowledgeable about this subject?" Zeto asked. "I mean I knew that places like this exist, but rarely do I ever hear or read about these places, the traps, the farms, the conditions."

"Let's just say I have a vested interest and read whatever I can get my hands on, especially after what happened to my father. Also, being that I hunt for myself, I need to be aware of the let's just say the *hunt-related hazards* that go along with it. If it looks like a duck and quacks like a duck, it's probably a duck. Bait follows the same line of logic. If it's too easy to get, it's probably bait, and all bait leads to traps."

"You hunt out there all alone?" He could not believe it.

"Either that, or I starve." She half laughed.

"But there are so many dangers. I didn't realize them all

until I was actually out there. I didn't realize a lot of things. If you were mine I would never let you out at night to hunt." *Did he just say that out loud?*

Adrianna's eyes grew round. She felt her heart skip a beat. She also noticed a, *I can't believe I said that,* expression working on his face. What does one say after that? She wanted to reach out and stoke his face. So she did the next best thing. She ignored it.

"I'm pretty good at it. I am always careful. Most of my food source is aquatic. I am not a big meat eater... clogs the arteries. I live more on poultry and seafood."

So "great swimmer" is also added to the list."

"You are going to have to show me this list...."

Before they had a chance to finish their conversation, Farmer Tucci came crunching back, his big heavy-duty work boots making large tracks in the snow. Zeto and Adrianna looked at each other as they were being lifted from the snow.

Had three hours passed already? Farmer Tucci was unusually quiet. Not his loud obnoxious self. He carried their cages back inside but the order had changed. Zeto and Mooch were now sandwiched between Adrianna and Marcellina and Venanzio, Castore and Fidele followed by Edna and Simone. Directly across from him were Beppe, Santo and Teo, followed by Frank and Dominic, then the newlywed Caterina and Renzo, and finally Auturo, Enzo and Plino, the three quiet ones that rarely murmured a word.

Zeto's eyes adjusted to the dingy shed. He wondered what triggered this sharper image? He could see everyone and everything, in detail as though he was standing in bright sunlight. Of course the room wasn't washed in blackness, but the blistery winter day was cloud covered, so very little light squeezed through the shed's slats. The shed door swung open with a loud bang. Grumbling to himself, Farmer Tucci set his five gallons of food, something ground and smelling faintly familiar on the ground. What was it that he smelled? Something like the rabbit he had once smelled simmering in red wine.

His chef, a native of Naples made some kind of braised rabbit with sage polenta', not a favorite, but that unforgettable rabbit smell simmering so long in the pot permeated the entire downstairs, and he now was able to pick up a whiff of that same scent now. Was he scenting again? What was happening to him? Sight? Smell? He looked up in surprise.

"Eat your breakfast. Healthy minks have healthy fur." He made another guttural sound as he began scooping ground up rabbit. Zeto was pretty sure it was rabbit. Tucci bent down and shoved the food draw back toward Zeto. A large mound of toxic waste loomed in front of him.

"Don't ever get married." Farmer Tucci said with venom. "I thought I was marrying Snow White and I ended up with the Wicked Witch. Do this. Do that. Nag. Nag. Nag. Never satisfied. Always breaking my hump to keep her happy. Whining about this. Never any peace." He shoved more ground up slop into trays, mumbling and complaining until he swiveled around; head bent and stomped out of the shed.

A hushed stillness filled the shed. Everyone stood looking around at each other when suddenly, simultaneously and without any pre-thought, everyone burst out into roaring laughter, violent hilarity at the performance they had just witnessed.

When the laughter finally died down, Venanzio, always quick with a ready quip said, "Like, do you even think the Wicked Witch would want that bloated piece of work, like wasn't she kinda smart you know, like making a regular apple into a poison one? Like, I would think that would take a certain amount of brain activity." More laughter ensued. "Like I mean it, what's so funny, man? The dude is like really out there. As nasty as an old canker sore."

"Oh Venanzo," Adrianna said through each giggle, "Please stop... Can't laugh anymore... my bell... my belly is beginning to hurt."

Zeto watched them all especially Adrianna. Her laughter made his heart soar and his spirits to lighten. When the laughter stopped once again, they all began to eat.

Mooch looked over at Zeto, chewing with care. When he swallowed he said, "You have got to eat something. You'll starve."

Zeto looked at the deposited heap of sludge with both hunger and repulsion. "I really do not think I will be able to get that down."

"Don't think about it. Just open your mouth and swallow.

130

There is really nothing to chew anyway. Watch me."

Zeto watched Mooch take a bite at it, eating it like a dog, and then swallow. "I didn't chew anything. Just grab and swallow."

"As I said before, you are a professional eater. You could make a living out of eating and make a fortune. Unfortunately I am not."

"That may be true," Mooch said sadly, "but it really is not that bad. Just try it. You have to eat something."

Adrianna voice floated into his ears. "He's right. You have to get something in you. You are going to need all the nutrients you can get and although this is not gourmet cuisine, it is protein and you are going to need all the protein you can get. Please. If I can do it, so can you."

Zeto could not argue with that. He was hungry. Starving in fact. And she looked so worried about him. How could he continue to act like a stubborn spoiled mink?

He took a small pinch of the ground rabbit by his claw, took a deep breath, threw it to the back of his throat and swallowed.

Mooch smiled. "Now was that so bad?"

Zeto looked over at Adrianna who was still looking at him. "Yes. It is that bad, but I'll get through it."

...At that, all three of them began to eat.

Chapter Six

Digging

The Grand General sat in the Count of Ulderico's study drinking hot tea with the Contessa and her brother. Books, from ceiling to floor covered three walls, and a fireplace crackled in the center of the room. Every piece of furniture seemed oversized and masculine, richly textured rugs scattered over buff hardwood floors. The room was dark, except for small wall sconces strategically placed; fire from the fireplace danced off the Contessa's face, illuminating it as she sat sipping her tea and listening to her brother Angelo report all their findings from the last four days.

It had been many years since he had last seen Arabella. She looked tired, but mostly sad. When he was a young officer in the Royal Guard, he thought she was the most beautiful female mink he had ever seen. He imagined he had been in love with her then, but half of the minks at court and the ones guarding them were in love with her also.

She was easy to love. She dazzled everyone with her sparkling beauty. But her heart is what flocked everyone to her side. A heart that cared enough for everyone, no matter their station, one that had touched a young officer of the Royal Guard by taking his hand one enchanted evening, and leading him out onto a ballroom dance floor to waltz the night away. He wondered if she remembered? Had he been more confident, more like Salvo, she would have been his wife and there was a time when he thought she would have accepted. It would be his son they were sitting here discussing. But Salvo Ulderico held all the cards, had all the credentials. A Viscount versus a mere royal officer? Actually it was no contest.

He had been out of the country when Salvo died. And today, she needed him to bring her son back to her, their son if circumstances had been different. He had remained a crotchety old bachelor. After her, well, that was just too hard an act for anyone to follow. But he had a good life, moved up the ranks of the MIA. Became Grand Deputy, then Grand General and Royal Minister of Defense of the Mink Military.

He supposed he came a long way fast and never looked back, until two days ago when he received word from H.R.H. Prince Montaga that they had a situation on their hands. He could have sent someone else to do this job, but for a reason he couldn't put his claw on, he wanted to handle it personally and here he was sipping tea across from the only female mink he had ever loved....

"So, as I understand it," the Grand General flipped open a notebook, "he has been scented, 3.2 kilometers away, 1.3 from a location at the foot of the Apennines called Road Kill, and interviews generated from individuals in attendance that night described an altercation between Muccino Alberdini, and another male mink playing in a band, by the way, his name, I have it right here, hold on...." The Grand General shuffled through his notebook of notes, "Oh, here it is, a Rocco Fiore, apparently over a female mink.

During Mr. Fiore's interrogation he denied any devious misconduct claiming that he and other members of his group took chase for approximately a kilometer before they stopped due to a contractual performance they had made with the owner of Road Kill. He claimed that near the 1.0 kilometer point he and other members of his band, who have also been questioned, decided to discontinue the chase because they would have had to forfeit payment for a night's work. The interviewers accepted Mr. Fiore's explanation because no trace scents of any altercation were tracked.

They did, however, track a glandular release from Muccino Alberdini, at 1.03 kilometers from Road Kill, but nothing that drew suspicions of foul play. Their trace scent was then followed along a tributary of the Tiber, 1.3 kilometers, making their location approximately 3.2 kilometers from here, which by the way, had they cut across that channel, it would have shaved 2.0 kilometers off their travel time. That is one fact in the report that puzzles me. Why did they not swim across? It would have been a very easy feat...."

"Zeto cannot swim." Contessa Arabella interrupted softly.

The General surprised, looked up from his notebook and their eyes met. The look on her face stopped him dead in his tracks. "Then, let me continue. A strong scent was traced near a large deciduous tree, the officers wrote "Beech Tree," with a question mark after it, and that is about all we have.

There were no continued scents from that locale. I am not

exactly sure what happened there, but I have a COBRA unit arriving in the morning and they should be able to answer most of our questions."

"COBRA?" Angelo asked. "I have never heard of such a unit."

The Grand General looked over at both of them, brother and sister. They had long finished their tea. "COBRA is a special task force. COBRA is an acronym for "Covert Operative Bureau of Rescue and Attack."

He paused. "Let us just say that the general mink population has no knowledge about them and we like it that way. These minks have been trained to become invisible to any environment, and scent. Their scenting abilities rank highest in the world. I plan to detail a unit consisting of 75 soldiers tomorrow to cover over a 16 kilometer radius of woodland near or around key areas.

We will know then exactly what happened and take it from there. These soldiers go in. They get the job done. No one is aware of their presence until it is over. They are as silent as a snake and as deadly as cobras. But in the meantime, there is much work to be done, so I must be going."

The Grand General rose from his seat, "It was nice to meet you Signor DiLuca," he looked over to Angelo. "Contessa," He bowed his head toward her.

Arabella turned to her brother. "Sit, Angelo, I will walk

the Grand General to the door."

Together they walked toward the entrance hall, where a footmink opened front thick double doors. A cold black wintry night greeted them. He turned to face the Contessa. "I will do everything in my power to bring your son back."

"I know you will, Tito." Her lips curved into a cheerless smile.

"You remember?" He asked.

"How could I forget you Tito? I know it has been a long time, but who ever forgets their first love?"

Hearing this was something unexpected. He had never known. He looked down at her and smiled. "Arabell, you always did have a tendency to throw me off my guard, as a young soldier, and now, even as an old one."

"Please Tito, you must find my son. You must." She took hold of his fore paws. "Promise me you will do everything you can to find him and bring him home."

He looked down at their clasped paws. "Lady Arabell, I will not rest until you have your son safely back home." With that he turned and walked out into the night.

***

Mooch sat watching and listening; the element of observation was amazing once you learned to keep your trap shut. And he was keeping his shut. He noticed things, things he would

137

normally have missed had he been flapping away at the mouth. Zeto was changing. Each day he watched him and each day he noticed this change a little more. For one thing, he no longer played *"Blind Man Bluff."* He could see almost as well as he did and he had always considered his night vision superior.

He may have exaggerated just a tad upon his other physical attributes, maybe made himself appear somewhat more honed and skilled than he actually was, but he wasn't lying about his ability to see at night and being that Zeto was almost totally enshrouded in darkness in here, he could see that he was quickly catching up.

He also noticed that Zeto could smell what Tucci was bringing them for meals before the shed door ever opened. He knew that he sometimes mixed ground fish parts in with their rabbit. He could overhear conversations in the last cage down. Of course that was no great feat, except they were the married couple Renzo and Caterina, whispering to each other. He knew Zeto heard entire conversations because he laughed when he heard her say something amusing or witty to her husband, and sighed when her husband murmured reassurances that they would find a way out.

There was one more thing that Mooch noticed, grander than the other three. He noticed life in Zeto's eyes, as though there was a real live mink living inside him now, something that he had never seen before, and he had spent a great deal of time with Zeto to notice that difference. His personality usually flat and formal, became more relaxed and light-hearted, even animated. And yesterday he began to talk to him again, and surprisingly enough, with civility. His tongue no longer pierced him with barbs and sarcasm. He no longer knifed him with dagger looks. Not that he didn't deserve every stab.

Mooch took complete responsibility for their present situation, and was grateful that he had been forgiven. The old Zeto would have held a grudge until his dying day. ...Gone to his grave still clutching onto it. Not this Zeto. He had never seen him this way. Many of his old friends had been discarded for lesser offenses.

Even though they faced a life-threatening situation, it appeared that he was smiling and laughed easier.... At first he could not understand it. It didn't make sense. But then when he looked, took a really good look, he also saw something else that he had never seen in Zeto before. He saw want in his eyes. Mooch smiled. *This was so great!* He had waited a long time for this to come, but never was sure that it would. This was the quintessential mink that never wanted for anything, and Mooch had known him a long, long time.

Locked up, caged in with all his luxuries stripped away and what...no complaining, no moaning or whining, oh no, he wasn't wanting for those things. No grumbling... being cooperative and even optimistic? This wasn't the Zeto he had known all these years. No siree.

If he were a betting mink, which he wasn't, but if he were, he would bet that Zeto hadn't thought about any of his so-called *can't live without* comforts, let alone miss any of them. He would bet that he had not thought about his world of prestige and privilege.

Not one mention of one drop of those fancy wines of his that lined the walls of his wine cellar that he liked to brag about…oh no… or dinner parties that he attended, or the scrumptious cuisine prepared by one of the top Italian chef's in all of Europe.

It was Mooch who was dreaming about them, reminisced about all those delightful meals he had eaten there, that was for sure, but not Zeto. Zeto wasn't missing anything, did not once mention his big warm soft bed or that stupid family album he jammed down everybody's throat. When Mooch thought back on it, he realized that Zeto hadn't complained once about the conditions or all the discomfort of being crammed in a cage, because Zeto wanted something, and what he wanted, was *her*.

Mooch looked over at the two of them whispering in low voices *as though he couldn't hear*. He pretended to be asleep most of the time when they talked quietly about their lives, but he wasn't. He was listening to every word, tone and chirpy sigh. He knew that Zeto had finally met his match. This was one female that could not be bought, sold or traded. He smiled with his eyes closed just listening to their gentle banter. He thought that this was going to be either Zeto's downfall or his deliverance, but he had a funny feeling it would be the latter. That was the born optimist in him thinking and he truly looked at brighter days ahead.

Zeto wanted her because the stupid jerk had fallen in love, from what he could see, from the very first day. It happened to him a couple of times, he was always falling in love, but with Zeto knowing him the way he did, he knew that this was the real McCoy, the real deal, and that it would happen for him only once.

He wondered if Zeto had realized it yet? Mooch sighed and tried to get comfortable. He found that his belly blubber, his extra tire, was coming in handy. *Fat is where it's at...* He yawned and turned on his side. He wanted to sleep. Yearned to sleep to relieve some of the boredom.

These days, he was passing his time listening. The three amigos' next door were sure making a racket with the mesh wire and sleep had become difficult lately. But he wasn't complaining. Hey... he was happy to be alive. He closed his eyes praying to dream about roasted duck, rabbit cacciatore and frog shish kabobs. Oooooooo... and muskrat pie!"

Zeto and Adrianna covered about every subject under the sun. In just four short days, he felt as though he had known her his entire life. They never ran out of things to say, to talk about.

They talked and talked and never stopped talking. She fascinated him on all levels. She had the three B's... He was beginning to believe that the three B's was just and another urban legend until he met her and there it was in plain sight. Right in front of him... The three B's. Beauty. Brains. Brawn. She had it all.

She had so many causes that encompassed just about every social and political compass, heck there were environmental forums that she was equally involved in. He wondered when she had time to work? She put herself out there. Got involved in issues that were close to her heart. Got in there, got her hands dirty.

Her mind and education at first had intimidated him, simply because the female minks in his social circles were brainless twits with nothing to offer, but a pretty face and all of this was new to him, something he had never experienced before.

It was fascinating to watch her face light up when she spoke; her passion and raw conviction emblazoned every nuance of her face, and thus stimulated him to think about all the possible points and issues she spoke of, things that he had never considered before.

And she never batted her eyes at him once, or acted the coy little minx. She spoke directly, was to the point and open, and a *gale of fresh air*. Air that took his breath away. He had never met anyone like her. She made him feel alive in this place of death, and for the first time in his life he felt that if given another chance, he would go back and do things differently.

Somehow she had changed him. He was in a position to create change in some of the social and political reforms that she spoke about. If they got out, there were many changes he was going to make, starting with himself and the thought of that excited him. She excited him. Sometimes he watched her while she slept, like he was right now, her little niece curled up beside her. He thought what an excellent mother she would someday make. The more he knew about her, the more he wanted to know. He was growing attached.

"Jezz dude, like check you out?" Venanzio said as he

watched Fidele pull yet another piece of steel from the bottom of the cage. "You're like razor teeth man."

Fidele spit out a small sliver of steel from his mouth. "I am like, you know, a walking billboard for milk." He looked over at Castore. "Yo dawg, get your skinny butt over here and see if you can fit your head and shoulders through this. If you can, we are in businessman. It's like fi-neeeee-co!"

Castore looked down at the small hole. "Already?" He stuck his head into the hole in the bottom of their cage, and slowly eased his shoulder down through. "You da man Fidele." He pulled himself back up. "All riiiiiiiiiiight, gimmeeeeee five."

Castore, Venanazio, and Fidele all high fived it.

"Yo everyone, listen up" Fidele yelled, "this hole is like done man. Castore can fit through it."

The shed suddenly awoke, became alive. Everyone broke out into hoots, hollers and cheers. The three teenage minks stood in their cramped cage with fore arms raised above their scrunched over heads, like three prize boxers, paws clasped, turning round and round to face their audience.

Beppe clutched the mesh of his cage. "Castore it is up to you now. We have got to do this right, because there are no second chances. Squeeze down through and there should be an opening at the far end of this shelving if it is anything like the opening in the front. Be careful not to step in any lime. You'll track it. Then I want you to climb up the back and walk down the outer shelf and open up Count Ulderico's cage and then Frank and Dominic's. We can't all be freed.

He turned his head to the other cages. "Listen everyone. Just because we are working through the night does not give us a guarantees that Signor Tucci won't suddenly show up. I don't trust that man. He's rabid. The fewer down there, the better. The three of you can take turns digging through."

"I think the three of us can handle the digging, but with the ground as frozen as it is, I don't think we can do it all in one night Signor Bepe." Zeto shook his head and began rubbing the white fur around his mouth. He felt jittery.

"I agree," Frank said. "We'll be workin' in shifts, but I don't think we're going to able to tunnel under this baby in one night. We won't know until we get down there."

"Well, do the best you can," said Beppe. "Castore it is up to you now."

Dominic patted Frank on the back. "Castore, this is your show. You can do this..."

An electric atmosphere filled the shed as Castore stuck his head and shoulders down through the small hole that all three of them, but mostly Fidele, had made. Castore was small for his age and schoolyard bullies had a field day inflicting their special bully talents on him daily until two miracles showed up one day as though they had been sent from God. One was named Venanzio and the other Fidele. The two toughest minks in the school and they had picked him to be their friend for reasons he had never been able to figure out. The three of them had become fast friends, inseparable, and no one taunted or called him names again.

He had grown up in a house full of strapping male minks and his father had constantly pushed him toward contact sport oriented activities, which he failed at miserably. He hated that he was small-boned and short in stature. He used to measure himself weekly when he was younger. His mother told him that he would *shoot up like a weed* when his hormones kicked in, but that hadn't happened either. But today, staring down into this hole, he felt larger than life. It was the first time in his life he felt blessed to be little. He would do this no matter what he faced on the bottom.

"Ewww....Ooooooooooo" Castore choked. He could not breathe. He tried to watch where he was walking. He yelled up, "Oh man, this is like some really nasty stuff down here. Like totally crappy, I mean it man, and it's like everywhere."

Venanzio and Fidele broke out into laughter. "Watch where you're stepping dude," Venanzio shouted, "we like have to live with your stanky butt."

Beppe shook his head and frowned over at the two. "Venanzio. Fidele. Not now."

He looked at the small mink below them. "Castore, I told you it would not be pleasant."

"Holy Cow!" They could all hear Castore down below the hole moving about on the ground. "My hind legs like don't want to work man. Gimme a minute to work my muscles. Gotta cramp. Being inside that stupid box has like totally reeked havoc my body man. Ain't nothing wantin to work."

He wrinkled his nose. "Hey, I could use a gas mask too. Anybody up there got a gas mask to throw down? I could use some high boots too. Man, this stuff is funky."

They all sat in their cages listening to Castore clamoring around below them in the hay. "Holy Crapola it's a good thing we can all see in the dark, cause this is too much," then the sound of movement and finally, he reappeared on the shelf next to their cages.

"Dude, like quit your whining man, like what'd you expect, shined up parquet floors?" Venanzio said.

"Whoa, like that is a crud hole, a cesspool man. I didn't expect that. I'd rather smell Fidele's farts all night than smell that again. We could write a book after this experience and call it the *The Poop Fields.*"

"Dude, like...." Venanzio began, "like some human already wrote a book like that called *The Onion Fields* and the…"

"Castore, hurry," Zeto said impatiently. "Let me out of here." He looked over at Adrianna who sat starring up at him. She smiled at him and he thought, *"Your kingdom of dreams awaits."* He smiled back at her and looked over at Mooch who was standing in the corner with that goofy grin not saying a word.

Castore walked carefully down the wooded plank until he reached the front of Zeto's cage door. His claws were trembling. "Okay, man, I'm cool. Let me see how to remove this clasp."

He pulled down on the metal fixture for a few moments. No movement. "Oh, I see how this works. Once I slide this stupid pin over, I think I can pull this latch up and the door will open."

As still as statues, everyone watched, waited, held their breath and prayed. He concentrated and worked the steel pin and suddenly everyone heard that familiar click as the pin slid out of the latch.

"Whoa, man." Everyone applauded, and Castore's face reddened under his fur.

He turned his attention back to the door. "Now let me concentrate on getting this handle up. When I do that man, I gotta get outta the way, cause this cage door is going to spring open, like pronto"

Another hush descended upon the group. They waited, listening and watching. Castore struggled with the handle, but within a moment's time he scurried to the left as the cage door sprung open.

...The minks went wild as Zeto stepped out of his prison. Mooch followed close behind only to stretch his limbs that were stiff and cramped. All of them, pushed against their cages watching. Zeto worked his hind legs back and forth and then walked carefully along the outer edge with Castore following him. He walked in front of Frank and Dominic's cage door, worked on the pin over and released the latch and within seconds their door sprung open.

Another round of cheers and applauds filtered through out the room. Everyone's spirits soared. All three minks climbed down while Castore waited on top. The plan as was previously devised was to keep Castore up while the other three went down, this way it would be easier for him to lock them back up when they finished for the night, or if they had to scurry quickly back into their cages in the event that Tucci unexpectedly made an appearance, so he sat down on the end of the ledge kicking his hind legs and waited.

They descended upon the far wall that butted up against a corner. They all felt that this area would be the least obvious place for Tucci to discover anything from any vantage point in the shed, even if he decided to change the hay, which to their knowledge, he had done only once, the location they had all decided upon would not be in his line of vision.

Although they planned to fill the hole when they finished digging with a little hay and some loose dirt to hide their work, they were aware that they could be caught at any time.

Speed digging was of the upmost importance. Zeto, Frank, and Dominic were very careful to stay clear of the lime; however, a thin band of it lay across where the shed wall met the dirt. Zeto used his claws to scratch it away, while Frank and Dominic carried it into the hay to bury it.

Zeto was the first to begin the digging. The top layer of earth would be more challenging since it would be more frozen than the layers beneath. Zeto made several attempts to puncture the ground with his front three strongest claws, but with each attempt he came up with nothing.

Maybe this would be another failed body function. He had never used his claws for manual labor, and using them kept them sharp. *"Your kingdom of dreams awaits."* Zeto looked down at the scratching marks he had made. *"Your kingdom of dreams awaits."*

He raised his right fore arm into the air and in a perfect arc, swung down throwing every cell in his body into those three claws. When he tried to bring them back up, he discovered they were stuck. Looking down, he saw that he had breached the frozen dirt. He closed his eyes and said a silent prayer. He pulled back with all the strength God had given him and relief spread through him as a large chunk of dirt came with it.

As soon as he brought it up, Frank and Dominic were there to haul it to the side and break it down into soft granular particles. And so the process of digging began....

...Before dawn, all were tucked safely back into their cages. They had dug through most of the night and had made more progress than they thought possible. They had taken turns and had tunneled to the other side. Zeto had thought the shed walls were thicker. It turned out that they were so thin that the next step down would have been Plywood. No wonder they were freezing to death in this place of unending darkness.

His eyesight at night still amazed him. He could see almost everything, as if he were looking through the lens of a giant magnifying glass. Sometimes it was hard to believe. He had no idea what he had missed all these years. He had been blind in more ways than one. At the thought, he looked over at Adrianna. What he had been missing? She was what he had been missing.

She was sleeping now, soundly with her niece curled up

next to her. His heart began to race as he looked at her long black lashes resting across her upper cheeks. What was this feeling? What was welling up inside him...? His heart picked up more speed. He felt every beat, every drop of perspiration, a gentle trembling. His paws were slightly clammy. Was it that simple? *Love?* Could he love her? Love her?

...God, oh God... *Love?* Zeto gulped hard as a panic shot through his body, a swift plunge of something dropping to his gut. *Love?* How could it be love? How could he love anyone in five days? It was madness, complete and total madness, it had to be. But then, when he looked back over at her, he knew with a calm finality, that this was all providence, the way it was intended it to be. That he was brought here under unusual circumstances to meet her, to fall in love with her, and by God, to live happily ever after with her.

He sat in his cage listening to Mooch snore. He sat for a long time pulling at his whiskers, and thinking and thinking some more and finally making plans, when exhaustion overtook him and he finally fell asleep...

Every one of them was dead tired the next morning. All of them had sat in their cages and had waited, sat up the entire night to hear the news that they had broken through to the other side. "*Hope springs eternal.*" Now he knew what it meant. Before leaving, they stuffed the tunnel with hay and soft soil, soil they had crumbled to the consistency of sand. Zeto knew that tonight after their last feeding, when total blackness approached this little shed, and all was quiet, that he had to be the one that had to leave.

It made perfect sense. He would follow along the graveled road out, but hidden in the woods and he would keep going until he found his guards or they found him. He knew that he no longer smelled the same. He hadn't been able to bathe in six days. He would kill Tucci if one tiny flea infested his fur. But his men were pros and they would be able to smell deep beneath the stench.

No one mentioned who was to leave since the day the two of them had arrived, the same day he had emphatically told all of them to go pound it, that it would not, under any circumstances, be him. But much had changed in a week. He had changed. His abilities had changed. He would go and nothing would hold him back. He would tell everyone of his plans tonight, right before he left.

***

The Grand General stood in front of 75 COBRA soldiers, all standing tall and at attention as dawn broke over the horizon. He had worked with this group and their unit commander, Colonel Lugasteino, on many missions. These 75 were the best of the best, a task force in both ground and aquatic warfare. He had handpicked each one of them. He stood in front of Ulderico Palace, facing all 75 ready to brief them.

The commando leader stood two meters in front of the rest.

"The mission I am about send you on is personal. I have hand picked each and every one of you from various squadron task units to build and mold and train you into the most elite group of soldiers in the world. You are considered matchless, and peerless, and because you are both, you must live up to that which has made you the soldiers you have become. Precision geographics and facilitated trail retrieval are expected. Failure is never an option. Mastery over the enemy. Your job is to scent Count Ulderico, then track the enemy. And there is an enemy out there. In all such cases, there is always an enemy.

As your COBRA code and creed which I created states, that all of you are to lead, follow and never quit, to serve His Majesty's Army with honor, integrity, and loyalty, with expectation of victory. I expect that from all of you today. With haste, we need to find out what happened to Count Zeto Pantaleone Ulderico, and where to retrieve him. Last location, 3.2 kilometers from our present position. He was tracked to a Beech Tree 20 meters from a Tiber River ravine, north by northwest."

He handed Colonel Luganstino an article of Zeto's clothing. "Colonel, you and your soldiers, scent this. Do not act until I have had a chance to debrief you. The Ulderico family has sentinel guards and soldiers of their own in the surrounding perimeters. They are there to assist you. Until we know what we are facing, do not act unless a crisis situation should arise. Do you understand?"

Their squadron leader yelled, "Yes sir."

"One more thing. Do not fail me."

Colonel Luganstino saluted, stiffly turned and walked back into his regiment. "Dismissed."

All saluted their Grand General, *Capo S.M. Difesa*, turned simultaneously and started toward the forest.

Zeto had catnapped for maybe an hour when the now familiar scent of ground rabbit reached his unobstructed naval cavities. He slowly opened his eyes. He still had a hard time believing he could see in the dark, hear even the faintest of whispers, and could actually smell anything that was this cold and this raw. Cold and raw? Just as the thought crossed his mind, Farmer Tucci burst through the shed door carrying the familiar rabbit heaped bucket, and whistling a tune.

"Good morning my little bambinos." He placed the bucket down next to his right booted foot. Zeto could see the large scooper shoved deep into the rounded top. ...Another meal of slop.

"And it is a good morning, you little groggy sleepy heads. Today we eat first and then outside we go to get a breath of that clean, cold fresh air. Gotta keep those furry little coats of yours growing, especially you." He pointed to Mooch.

"What happened to your shiny coat their little buddy? Got a bad case of the *mange*?" He chucked as all eyes turned to Mooch. "I can't use that now can I? Who would want a pelt like that on an expensive full-length mink coat? What am I gonna do with you...I want you for your coat Mr. Minko, not your blubber. My, you are a chubby one aren't you? But, we can't slack off now can we?"

He began the scooping ritual. "Eat-um up. Gotta keep all of you healthy. Wouldn't want any of you to get sick on me, now would I?"

What Zeto wouldn't give at that moment to change into an adult human male? The thought made him tremble at the violence he would heap upon this bloated oaf. Everyone ate in silence, except Mooch, who sat in the corner of his cage, looking pitiful.

Zeto turned to Mooch and said, "You need to eat some of this."

"Honestly, Zeto, I'm really not hungry... but you go ahead."

"You can't honestly take to heart what that simpleton said." Zeto grimaced. "The man is an absolute lunatic and you know it!"

"He is," Adrianna exclaimed. "I told you that on the day the two of you arrived. He's a stupid dangerous human. Please Mooch; take nothing he says to heart. Please eat something."

Mooch pasted a weak smile on his face, but his humiliation was too acute that even a weak one was hard to conjure up.

Zeto decided that he wasn't hungry anymore either. Trying to eat and being forced to listen to this buffoon's asinine comments at the same time, was making him lose his appetite, but he knew that he had to eat because he didn't know when he would be able to eat again after he left this place. He acquired his natural abilities, but he knew in his heart that he would never be able to *hunt*. The thought of it sickened him.

"I'll be back in a few. Hurry and eat because outside we go."

"Hey," Tucci turned around at the shed door. "You guys are starting to stink. Someone told me that Benjamin Franklin, that American fellow used to take daily *air baths*. Yeah, for an hour a day. I wonder if it worked for him, because it surely isn't working for the bunch of you. Peeeeee-yewwww!!!" At that he laughed a little more, turned and closed the shed door behind him.

"Ooooooooooo.... I hate that man!!!" Edna, who hadn't said but two words in the six days of their stay, blurted out. "That man is incorrigible." Little Samone scurried over to her mother's side and put both fore paws around her waist. "And Signor Alberdini... if you believe anything that stupid human said then, shame on you!" Now everyone had stopped eating, jolted at the tone and volume of her voice. "From the moment you walked in here, I thought you were one of the most handsome males I have ever seen. So there now." She nodded, and crossed thick fore arms in front of her, almost daring anyone to contradict her.

Mooch, who was never at a loss for words, sat stunned, speechless.

"Dude," Venanzio rattled the wire on his mesh cage, "that man, is like dead meat if I ever get outta here.... Like I am going to spring up on that ugly cheesin' face of his and...."

"Stop." Mooch put his paw up. "I get the picture Ven, and thank you."

He turned and looked over at Edna who was still dripping with anger and added, "And Signora Edna, you have made my day more than I could ever tell you. A sincere thank you."

"You're welcome." She was already ambling back to her bowl. "And I meant every word of it."

"When we get out of here, there is a place called Crabby's that I would feel honored to take you and your little girl. They make the best crab cakes this side of the Tiber. You do like crab cakes don't you?"

"What mink doesn't love crab? And yes, we will be honored to accompany you...."

Zeto rolled his eyes and forced himself to eat. While Mooch rambled about Crabby's and his precious crab cakes, he was making more plans....

* * * *

Chapter Seven

The Great Escape

To ward off the frigid air that crept into every nook and cranny and marrow of his bones, Zeto rubbed both palms of his paws together in a vigorous back and forth motion and turned them upward so he could expel a warm breath into them.

He had never been exposed to the outdoor elements as he had over the past seven days. He could see bursting cones of warm breath shooting from all their noses. He could see that Mooch was once again asleep. He wondered how he could sleep in these freezing temperatures. He felt certain that if he fell asleep out here, he would never wake up. His gaze wandered over to Adrianna. He watched while she wrapped her tail around her niece. It was even colder today.

"This has got to stop." She looked down at Marcellina and then over at Zeto. "I don't know how much more of this she can take."

"Just be patient." He replied. He experienced the familiar surge of blood throughout his body, speeding heart rate, elevated blood pressure.

"I just worry about her. She is just a little minky." She reached down and touched Marcellina's head. "I hope she doesn't catch a chill. That would be all I need. I also worry about the scars, the psychological scars she will be left with if we get out of here."

"*When.*" Zeto corrected her.

"Yes. I forgot. When."

She smiled into his curious eyes for a moment. There was something different there. "What?"

"I don't believe I said anything." He broke out into that crooked grin she found so irresistible.

"I know. But you were thinking about something. You have that look in your eyes."

"What look?" He mocked. "There wasn't a single thought in my head."

"Now I *know* your fibbing. That will be the day when you have nothing going on in that head of yours. That brain of yours toils in perpetuity."

"Lady, you think you know me so well in only a week's time… to know when I have something on my mind?" Again, that lopsided grin. "And I like that word *perpetuity*."

"Your face has become easy to read." She said as she carefully studied it.

"And yours isn't. I never know what you are thinking. I would give up everything, title and everything that went with it to get inside that brain of yours, which by the way is a very good brain, for just one day."

"Well, thank God you can't." She laughed.

"I *was* thinking about something," he admitted sheepishly. "And it did have something to do with you."

"Oh, you are so secretive this morning, my Lord. And pray tell, what would be on your mind concerning me?"

160

She had grown accustomed to his soft creamy voice and dark eyes, eyes that twinkled sometimes with mirth; and their light bantering. Had he any idea what she felt for him, he would run screaming. No. He would never learn her heart. They were from two different worlds, places that were polar miles apart.

"That you will someday make an excellent mother. That also made my list." She wasn't prepared for that comment. It took her by surprise and almost rendered her speechless.

Zeto could see that he had startled her. For a second, he didn't think she was going to respond.

"Motherhood is the greatest of all vocations. It's the hardest and lasts a lifetime, with no time off or overtime pay. But I imagine there are a lot of fringe benefits. I would like a job like that someday. Thank you. You probably think I am silly but...".

"I think you are *magnificent*." He looked into her eyes and felt everything bubbling to the surface, feelings he had come face to face with last night. He breathed in her fragrance. "You, my lady, are *dangerous*."

Recovering from the fluttering in her stomach and a sudden tightening in her chest, she managed to string a few words together to formulate a simple sentence. "I am dangerous? And why may I ask is that, sir Count?"

"Because you are the most beautiful mink I have ever seen, body and soul. Because you have awakened something that has been asleep for a long, long time. Because I am content to be locked in this cage forever if it means I get to spend forever with you." He

161

bent in closer and whispered, But most importantly Adriana, because I have fallen for you. I love you."

He could see that he had shocked her.

"Honestly I never had a chance. I was a goner from the moment I laid eyes on you." Never taking his eyes off her, he placed the palm of his paw against the flat surface of his cage, feeling his heart beating wildly waiting for her to take it all in and speak.

Stunned, for this was the last thing she thought would spring out of his mouth, Adrianna leaned against her cage for support, and placed her palm against his. "You honor me Count." Though shocked, she rummaged through her brain to find the right words. She knew what this was. She had read about it and now she was experiencing it first hand. If only it were true. If only she came from his world. If only he came from hers'. If only she hadn't met him here, in this world.

"I am but a mere teacher. My blood is not blue, but red. You are in an extremely stressful environment and sometimes in such environments as these; attachments form and become so real to us. But out there where reality awaits, attachments of such, rarely occur or keep."

"I realize this came to you unexpectedly, but am I to believe that you do not believe me?" He dropped his paw to his side; raw anger took over the tone in his voice. "That you think the feelings that I have just gutted from the deepest part of me are a result of some type of neurotic-stress syndrome from being a prisoner in here?"

"Unfortunately it does happen." Her voice barely whispered.

"Well it doesn't happen to me!" Zeto said incredulously. He stood before her, both paws clutched the wire between them. "I have met every female mink from all over Italy. They come from the best bloody families in all of Europe and they come in droves. Not one, did I ever give a second glance. Not one!

That first day here, the day I was brought into this miserable den of death, I could not keep my eyes off of you. I had just been imprisoned in a 2 x 4 cage fully aware of where I was and what I was facing and I couldn't keep my bloody eyes off of you, and you know Adrianna, even I use to think the color of someone's blood was important, but being in here has forced me to think clearly... more clearly than I have ever done in my life, and I have come to realize that it just doesn't matter. The color of your blood is the same color as mine and the way I feel about you will never change, in here..." He turned and pointed toward the woods... "or out there."

Adriana could not believe he was pursuing this. She didn't believe these were his true feelings for a second. She knew what this was. It happened all the time. Couldn't he just believe her and understand that what he was feeling may seem real to him, very real, but they weren't. Couldn't he grasp that she knew about these kinds of things? That she was well versed this area? Could he see that her heart was shattering; her hopes swallowed? He just wanted his way.

163

He wanted her to fall to her knee in romantic bliss when she knew in her heart that this was all a mirage. Like seeing water in the middle of a desert, and she would rather see dry sand today than to drink from a fresh cool fountain that quenched her thirst only to discover later that it never existed.

"From the first moment I met you," she burst, "I thought you arrogant and full of conceit, the kind of mink that snapped his fingers and everyone listened and obeyed. Spoiled and set in your ways. I knew your kind. And now... well, look at you. You turned everything around. You tell me that you care for me, and expect me to fall to the floor of this cage in a faint, or better yet to accept that what you are saying is true! How dare you tell me that you've fallen for me. How dare you!"

"And how dare you throw it back in my face!" Zeto spat.

"How can I throw something back if I never had it to begin with?" Her heart was beating so fast that she thought it might burst in her chest.

"Whether you want it or not, you definitely have it and forgive me madam for allowing my heart to speak to you. I was out of line. I actually thought you might return the feeling!" With that, Zeto turned and walked over to the far side of his cage and sat down with his back toward her.

He would never understand the female mind. What did she think he was, some Lothario spouting the same sentiments to every female mink he met? He never murmured those words to any other female mink in his life beside his mother, and he rarely told her.

164

She was his *inamorata*.

He sat and stewed over her words for quite a while... when a new thought occurred... she truly did not believe him! He had spoken in earnest, from a depth so deep in his soul and she didn't believe him? No. She didn't believe a word he said. She was convinced he was in the throes of some kind of weird cage neuroses.

Had she not felt the same, she would have told him at once, he knew this much about. Adrianna was open, a well educated female, comfortable with expressing her opinions and attitudes on just about any level. He stood up. He was going to *make* her believe him. The conversation was far from over. Somehow he would make her believe him. As he rose to march back over to get some answers, his cage was swung unexpectedly in the air. He had not seen or even heard it coming.

"It's freezing out here." Farmer Tucci said. "I can see those coats of yours growing as we speak." He looked in at Zeto, "And your fur, little buddy, that is about the best fur I have seen in... well... ever!"

He proceeded to carry their cages back into the shed. Zeto and Mooch held on while they were swung violently back and forth. He held on while they were placed in a new position toward the back of the shed.

Waiting for Tucci to reappear, he watched in disbelief as he brought in the next cage, Edna and her daughter Simone's, and placed it next to theirs. This could not be happening. Not now. He took a few deep breaths. Why had he lost his temper? He was Signor Cool under fire--remember? He should have stayed and talked this out with her, but instead, he had turned from her and walked away angry like the spoiled bratty mink she thought he was.

He had to convince her that what he felt today was true, as true as it would be tomorrow and the next day and the next day after that, and for the rest of his life. Why had he lost his temper? He very rarely ever lost his temper. He lost his temper because he was never in love before and this love business was making him act stupid.

He watched as Tucci brought the next cage back into the shed and the next cage and the next and still no sign of Adrianna. Finally, the last cage that came through the door and placed on the shelf by the entranceway was Adrianna's. Inside, he could see her, though her back was toward him, so he could not see her expression. But he could feel all the blood rush from his face when he heard little Marcellina say, "Why are you crying Aunty A? Did I do something bad?"

Adrianna's voice was full of sorrow. "No, my darling." She reached out and pulled little Marcellina onto her lap. "You could never do anything bad. You are such a good little minky, so brave and so sweet, I just love you with all my heart."

"Then why are you crying?" Marcellina snuggled closer.

"Sshhhh... let's whisper okay?" Adrianna began to speak very softly, "because I am very tired sweet one."

Adrianna wiped her eyes. "And because you shouldn't be

here. You're still so young and maybe I am also just a teeny tiny bit worried that when we are free, and we will be freed Marcellina, that this experience will continue to bother you and I don't want it to bother you so that you will be afraid to live your life."

"I won't be afraid Aunty. I promise. And I'm really not so scared; after all I Tinka here," she held up a one eyed rag doll that had seen better days, "and I have you to protect me."

"I will protect you my little darling. I will. I will never let anything or anybody hurt you." At that she laid her head down on the top of Marcellina's and the two of them grew quiet.

Well this was just great. He made her cry. *Zeto my boy, you can just congratulate yourself on making a female cry. Not just any female, but the female you spouted love to…*If only he could talk to her. Have a private moment with her to make her understand and believe that everything he had told her was true. He sat feeling his frustration build. This cell hadn't seemed so bad when she was in the cage next to him, but now it was unbearable, he felt caged in, like he was about to explode….

"Alriiiiiiiighty my little bambinos, the smelly poopoo in here has got to go." Zeto could see that he had a rake in his hand. Everyone must have noticed because suddenly everyone was standing and watching him as he started to rid the shed of the dirty hay that lay beneath them. They waited for him to discover the filled-in tunnel they had completed last night.

"This really stinks... hey whatta you guys eating?" He continued to rake. "You need a change in diet, maybe some ground duckling or venison for lunch and dinner. *Naaaaaaaaah*."

He snickered as he raked under their cages, then walked to the back area of the shed. Everyone held their breath. "Hey... what's that?" He walked around the shelving to the far corner of the shed next to the wall and bent over.

Zeto closed his eyes and shook his head. *Not now, please*, was all he had the time to think, when Farmer Tucci stood back up and held a metal object up to a bare bulb that hung from the ceiling. "Looky here! I was wondering where I lost that darn thing."

Zeto could see a small shiny object between his fat thumb and his fat index finger. Relief engulfed him. He sat down because his legs felt too weak to support him and listened as Tucci rambled on about some stupid nut and bolt that he had been searching for that came off the overhead fan. The ceiling fan? Zeto brushed the sweat from his brow, looking up at the overhead fan that never stopped humming for a moment. More determined now than ever, Zeto was ready to get everyone out. This had gone on long enough.

Farmer Tucci laid fresh hay under their cages and again everyone held their breath when he began to scatter it throughout the back. He walked to the front and turned as he stood at the entryway. "You know, I even make money from your poopoo. Well good day to you all. Make it a good one."

Sparks spitted against the cast iron grate in Zeto's study.

Alert, Contessa Arabella listened as the Grand General once again sat across from her and Angelo. A pounding in her chest began the minute he stepped into the vestibule. The Grand General rested his notebook on his lap. "I have just received word from Colonel Lugasteino. I am afraid I have some bad news, but also maybe some good."

The Contessa reached out and grabbed her brother's paw. He held onto it tightly.

"Ten of my men came back to report that they found the very last location of Signor Alberdini and your son. They scoured the forest region within a 16 kilometer radius and the last scent they lifted came from under the aforementioned Beech Tree where your men tracked them."

She felt a waving sensation in her stomach; she could hear her heart drum-rolling in her ears. "Then they found nothing new?"

"Yes Contessa, they did. It seems that what they picked up was the scent of metal. Steel to be exact. Steel is comprised of several mineral compounds. Iron is one and the other is carbon. When iron ore is heated with an alloying material such as a carbon to give it its strength, specific odors are present.

Strong steel odors were tracked to the exact location with Zeto and Alberdini. They were both at the same position at the same time. The time of the smells do not differ one from the other. It is our belief, I am afraid, that both have been caught in a trap. Not a leg-trap, those traps have an altogether different smell because there are other elements involved in their making. Also, those traps leave blood traces and none were found.

Strong steel mesh scents were tracked. My men picked up faint mesh prints off of a few leaves that had been underneath it. They were also tracked downstream again at 50-60 meters next to an old country road. There the scent vanished. We have reason to believe that they were removed from this location to a vehicle of some sort.

My men are exploring selective roadways, but tire rubber is difficult to distinguish because they are all collectively made of rubber and manifest the same scents. We can date it, and trace it to its manufacturers, but this would be like trying to find a needle in a haystack. I think we would end up with a lot of mink-hours and come up empty handed.

"Oh my Zeto!" She placed her head in her paws and began to softly cry.

Angelo put his forearm around her and she clutched to his shoulder. "Oh what will we do Angelo? Please Angelo, tell me this is all a bad dream and that I will wake up and find my son alive and well and... please tell me, somebody please...."

Angelo looked over at the Minister of Defense of the Royal Military, with pleading eyes. "Contessa," the Grand General said sternly. He could not bear to see her cry. "You must allow me finish...."

She dabbed at her eyes and looked up from under Angelo's arm. He could see her tears glistening, and a handkerchief clutched in her hand.

"After a lengthy debriefing with Colonel Lugansteino, we have both come to consider the possibility that both were taken to a Mink Farm."

"Oh Tito... No! Oh please, say it isn't so! *I can't bear this. Oh Tito, I can't bear this!"* She cried with no bridle. "Not that! I would rather he be prey and have it over with quickly, than that slow miserable.... *Oooooooooonooooo.*" Her hysterical sobs rang through the quiet room.

The Grand General jumped from his seat and bent down before her shaking sobbing body. "Listen to me Arabell. This is probably the best of the bad news we could receive. If they were taken to a mink farm, we'll find them." He reached down and lifted her chin with his paw. "We will find them and get them out, but you have got to *trust* me. You have got to be brave and trust me."

"I do Tito, *I do. I have always trusted you*," she sniffed.

"We will find the locations of all the mink farms in all of Italy if we have to. But we will find it. Do you believe me?" He watched as she nodded her head. "And when we do, I promise you that we will move into the human realm, and if I have my way, we will destroy it. *All of it*. Nothing will be left. But I need reinforcements. I need all of your minks, and your brother's.

Angelo, I need to make arrangements to get aid from the badgers, European Polecats, and the Wolverine tactic units, which are the vilest of all weasels, and I will bring in more Royal regiments. We must begin at once. We have no time to lose. I will contact H.R.H. Prince Montega. The last we spoke, he was leaving the ultimate decision of a full scale human invasion in my hands."

The Grand General stood and began to cross the room, when Contessa Arabella caught up with him. "Thank you Tito," she grasped both of his fore paws and lifted them to her lips and kissed them. "Thank you so very much."

At that, the Grand General, cleared his throat, took a deep breath and whispered, "Anything for you." He opened the study doors and walked out.

***

...Zeto stewed the entire day. That fan bothered him. Now that he knew that a nut and bolt had fallen off, he wondered if the entire thing might not just collapse and come crashing down smashing them to bits. The fact that Adrianna was on the other side of the aisle and at the very end and that she still had her back toward him bothered him. How could he speak to her before he left without making more of a spectacle of himself? He had done a pretty good job of it this afternoon. He had eaten both lunch and dinner and it bothered him that his hour grew near. It bothered him that no one, not even Beppe, brought up the subject of who would leave tonight. He was ready to explode.

"Castore!" he yelled. The rest of the minks lethargic from their supper, stirred. "Get down and come around and unlock my cage door this instant."

Well that got everybody's attention. The room came alive

with everybody trying to talk at once. Even Adrianna turned to look at him.

Castore, usually talkative, remained silent as he went down through the hole and reappeared in front of Zeto's cage.

"What is this all about, Sire?" Beppe asked.

"I am going." He announced.

"Oh no you can't do this," Adrianna said vigorously shaking her head.

"Watch me." Zeto said as Castore nervously fumbled with the lock.

"Please Zeto, just stop for a moment and listen to me. You cannot do this. Let someone else do this, someone who has had more experience with woodlands at night."

Zeto's cage door opened. Nobody moved. "Now lock it up and go back to your cage," he said. Then he moved down the planking to the floor and reappeared on the opposite shelf walking toward Adrianna' cage.

"Please Zeto," she said while watching him unlock her cage door. "Don't do this. Please don't do this." He pushed up on the handle and the door sprung open. For the first time, he looked at her with no steel mesh to obstruct his view. Nothing separated them....

Zeto grabbed her around her waist and pulled her up against him, he felt himself relax when her forearms began to encircle his neck. He looked into her eyes. Tears hung on their rims. He reached up and wiped them away.

"Everything I said to you this morning came from my heart. I said *forever*. I knew from the very first day in this rat hole, that forever was what I wanted from you. Do you understand?"

She murmured a weak, "yes."

The shed, plunged in darkness, was as silent as a tomb.

"I won't let anything happen to you. I'm going and I will come back for you. I will. Do you believe me?"

Another weak, "yes."

"I will come back for everyone. Do you understand why I am the one that has to go?"

She hesitated and then shrugged her shoulders.

"I can't trust anyone else with your life, because your life belongs to me now. If you care for me, even a little, you must believe that I can do this."

She looked into a pair of intense black eyes and reached up to touch his cheek. "I am afraid for you Zeto. I am so afraid because I love you."

"Then kiss me." She turned her face up to his and he closed his eyes to feel the softness of the lips he had only dreamt about. Applause shook the room, along with whistles and hoots.

Adrianna and Zeto laughed and rested their foreheads together. He turned to face all his fellow *inmates*. He would never refer to them as his *roommates* as Tucci did. That implied a certain element of free will.

"I will return for all of you. Gather as much of your fur off your hides as you can. I realize this is not molting season, but gather as much as you can, pull it out if you have to. When you have done so, Castore will collect it from your cages, Frank, Dominic can help, but get it in there. If Tucci is as brain deficient as we all believe him to be, he will believe that I am at the bottom of Mooch's stomach." Laughter rang. "We must hurry."

Zeto turned and looked once more at Adrianna, the one female mink in the entire world that he knew he would love forever. He raised his paw to her cheek and again to wipe a fallen tear. "If you cry you are telling me that you don't believe in me."

"I am just afraid for you Zeto. Afraid. I just found you too."

He smiled at that. He liked the way it made him feel. "I will be back." He kissed her mouth and before he turned to lock her back up in her cage, he whispered into her ear, "I love you and I won't fail."

He stepped back and locked her cage door.

She watched him back away. "You must be careful Zeto. You must watch the sky and the ground at the same time. You must stay in any high grass you can find and keep low to the ground."

He walked down the long plank of old wood and turned to look once more at every face that he had grown so fond of in so short a time. "I will be back."

His extended family, locked up like criminals in cramped

175

cages with no room to move or stretch or even scratch.

"I will be back. It may take two days... but I will come back and when I do, as God as my witness, not one slab of wood will remain standing." *These minks were apart of his family now. No one was going to hurt them. He wasn't about to allow Tucci to electrocute them or inject them with some dang insecticide. No. This evil would not continue.*

"...Castore, Frank, Dominic, cover the tunnel once I am out." Zeto turned and climbed down and stepped upon fresh hay. He walked over and moved all the loose dirt and hay out of his way, and in a matter of minutes, climbed down into the hole and then he was simply gone.

* * * *

Chapter Eight
The Call of the Wild

Z eto stood outside brushing lingering fragments of soil from his fur. He took a deep breath. Freezing air hit his lungs as he surveyed the surrounding area with vision as clear as glass. He could see his breath moving rapidly in front of him.

Slow down. Think. Steady your breathing. He had no idea in which direction to head. He moved away from the shed, advancing toward the open area where Farmer Tucci plopped their cages every morning, and stepped onto a graveled circular space.

He approached Tucci's tan pick-up truck sitting in front of a dilapidated garage and looked behind it at a long narrow dirt and gravel road that he and Mooch had been brought in on. He knew that this road led to the other paved one.

One step at a time. First this road, and then the next. He hoped that when he reached that road he would remember the direction in which they had come. He knew it was daylight when they were brought here, but he had been so agitated at the time that nothing about the road came to mind.

Zeto walked along the road for a few minutes, and then bolted behind squatted bushes that ran along its side. He stayed under an umbrella of frozen pine needles and branches. There was still snow on the ground that appeared in thick patches here and there.

He walked and sniffed the air, stopping to look behind him, looking overhead and around with each step he made. At this rate, it would take him forever to travel the approximated six or so kilometers. He picked up the pace a little and tried to move as fast as he could, making as little noise as possible. He did not need to be heard by whatever might be out there lurking, *stalking prey*. But he was not going to think about that now. It would make him crazy; muddle his thinking. He had to stay focused and keep moving.

His legs felt weak. They quivered under the weight of his body. They were heavy, cramped from their lack of use and exercise, but he could not think about that right now either. *He had to keep moving.*

He kept himself close to the berm of the road in order to see when it met the other road, the bumpy paved one. *He could do this. He had to do this.* His future was sitting in a cage back there, and he was going to get help and go back to get it. Nothing would keep him from doing so… nothing. So much was at stake.

Forward he walked, nothing in the sky, he heard nothing, not even a deer and no smells. So much silence? *That was a good thing, wasn't it?* He figured he was too close to the road to encounter much danger. That would happen when he had to go in deeper.

It was amazing to look at the surrounding trees and bushes that ran along the road, and actually see them. He saw them as well as he did with his day vision. He wondered if he would still need his reading glasses. How did this all happen? He would have to study this phenomenon once he was home and settled.

...*Home.* He thought about his mother and what she must be going through. Though his natural proclivity was to dwell and over-analyze, he was baffled that he hadn't thought about his home during much of his incarceration. He hoped that his Uncle Angelo had settled her, calmed her. As long as he could remember, his uncle had always had a sedate affect on his mother. His Uncle Angelo was the driving force behind his mother and it used to drive his father nuts. It perturbed him that his mother continued to call upon his uncle over the slightest of problems and counted on him so often after they were married, and after a while she stopped in order to keep the peace. His father just never understood that relationship, that Uncle Angelo was more father than brother to her. Even he could understand that, but not his father.

Her own papa' died when she was a young minky, and being that Uncle Angelo was the eldest and *the son,* the job of being head of the household fell upon his shoulders. He had very little time to build a life of his own outside of the family.

He had a mother and three younger sisters to provide for. And so he never married. No wife. No offspring. The family's continued affluence was up to him and he quadrupled it many times over. Poor sweet Uncle Angelo. He wondered if he had ever been in love, cared for someone when he was a young mink? Funny that he never thought about it before now. He hadn't thought about a lot of things before.

Since Adrianna, his brain now roamed all over the place.

He had never understood love, or the spell it cast. He had often wondered about it in the past. Contemplated it. He knew that many died for it, pined for it, and some even killed for it, but he never knew it to be so powerful an emotion. He grew anxious just thinking about her stuck in that small pen with her niece. He couldn't think about that. It would throw off his game and more so than any other time in his life, he needed to be on his game...sharp. Out there, *that* was the line between life and death. He walked onward; in this shadowy place with cold winds blistering around him, but his nervous energy and the rapid pace in which he now walked was beginning to make him sweat.

...Ahead, Zeto could see a *T* in the road and walked even faster until he was officially, what appeared to be, off Tucci's land. He stood facing the junction... looking to the left and then looking again to the right. He had to photograph this all in his memory so that he would be able to lead the others back to this place of death, or maybe they would be able to *scent* him back?

He really was new to how the whole thing worked, but one thing he did know, had always known, and that was that no mink could ever scent themselves.

He thought he remembered that they made a left coming in, but he was pretty emotional at the time yelling at Mooch who was in the midst of a meltdown. He thought it was a left, was pretty sure it was a left. He stood and tried to think. This one turn could be the deciding factor between success and failure; life and death for all of them including Adrianna so there was no margin for error.

He was almost certain Tucci had turned left because he remembered sitting across from Mooch when the turn came about, and could vaguely remember that he had been lurched forward which almost sent him onto Mooch's lap. That being the case, they had to have been making a left because the centrifugal force while turning the bend had caused his forward motion.

If they had come from the opposite direction, the right, then he would have fallen backward. Whew! This was getting pretty complicated. Was he over analyzing again? Over-thinking too much? But he had to be mistake free. He looked again at the junction and made the right. He could not stand here all night trying to decide. He was almost sure he was going in the correct direction. But it was the word *almost* that alarmed him.

...Zeto's steps were slow yet determined. Thinking and moving and deciding... With each step he began to doubt himself. Mooch had been useless in mapping this route for any of them. He claimed that at the time, his brain was, *discombobulated.* He could remember nothing, not even what direction they had come in from when they turned onto the graveled road. Zeto moved a little further into the woods, but was close enough to the edge to follow.

He wondered how long he had been walking. It seemed like hours, but he had never been good at figuring out time. Being impatient by nature, time always dragged for him. Yet, it amazed him at how fast this past week had flown by.

Stuffed into such a little compartment with an oversized Mooch taking most of the space, and no freedom of movement, one would think time had to be unbearable, but most of that time he spent talking about almost everything with Adrianna. He told her things he had never told a living soul. She had that way about her. He never knew there was a female mink out there like her and to have found her on a mink farm of all places. How uncanny.

She seemed to have been made especially for him. She was someone he looked forward to growing old with. He shook his head in disbelief as he walked along frozen weeds and tall grasses, pushing them aside as he made his way. It had been the best and the worst thing that had ever happened to him. Go figure....

He looked skyward. The sight momentarily stopped his breath. So that is what the moon looked like up close and personal? In his haste to get out, hadn't noticed it before. He stopped for a moment and gazed up at its near fullness. He could not believe he was an adult mink experiencing an almost full, waning moon for the very first time, and with his very own eyes. Of course he studied astronomy, the lunar phases in school and had seen many pictures, but to actually see it, right before him, suspended there, sent a thrill through him, oh and all the stars... there they were, blinking like sparkling diamonds scattered throughout the night sky, peeking through at intervals and the black outline of a bird.

...*Wow, a bird--a relatively large bird. Wide wingspan... soaring down...coming toward him... one that flew at night.... Quickly he shot down, and in a nanosecond, it collectively came together. His eyes scanned the distance. Tree. Due south. Hollow tree stump.*

Zeto sprang into action, automatically running zigzag instead of a straight line. He recalled his father telling him that if anything ran in a straight line they were nothing more than a sitting duck.

The automatic maneuver just popped into his head. Zigzagging made for a harder target. Zeto could feel the wind stirring around him as he dove into a deep cavity, hearing its beak snapping behind him and an unnerving shriek. He crawled all the way to the back and leaned back against the inside wall. His head fell onto his chest. His entire body shook, his heartbeat thumped against his temples.

If he hadn't been looking up at the moon, he would be *owl chow* right now. The shrieking became more and more distant as the owl flew further and further away. *Now what the heck was he suppose to do?* He took a deep breath and tried to think. *Use your head Zeto!* It's not like Eagle Owls made a lot of racket when they snatched their prey giving them a lot of notice or reaction time. It was a sneaky bugger. Its wings, as though they weren't moving at all, were soundless as it descended upon its purpose, the victim always realizing a second too late.

How long was he going to have to sit in here? Would it come back for him knowing that he was hiding inside? That one got away? Did they do that? Or, did they move on when an intended meal got away? Didn't they sometimes hunt in pairs, like a tag team? One drove prey to exhaustion while the other would go in for the kill. Was there another one waiting somewhere around the corner? He sat there trying to decide what to do. He closed his eyes and rested his head back against a cold solid mass of moss when a profound drowsiness seemed to overtake him. *Wouldn't that be nice?* What would it hurt if he just rested for a little while and slept? He had slept so little in the last week. Surely a little power nap wouldn't hurt?

Zeto sprang forward and opened his eyes as wide as they would go. What was he thinking? Thinking about sleeping when he had a job to accomplish and lives to save. He crawled to the aperture and stopped and sniffed the air outside. Did he actually think he would be able to smell an Eagle Owl ...or any fowl for that matter ...a fox, or a wolf? He had never smelled any of these animals before so how would he be able to determine the difference and what would their difference be?

They were all out to have him for dinner. He crawled out a little at a time. Sitting at the front of the opening, he studied the sky. *Nothing.* He walked around to the back. *Still nothing.* He ran on all fours to a group of thick evergreens and crawled under. Dried hard needles pricked at his palms. He sat, peeking out, trying to gather his bearings to find the darn road. There it was, right where he left it. Walking along the road would make him a walking target, so he decided the best way to travel was to scurry low to the ground and park himself under evergreens when given the chance.

Zeto had broken out of a mink farm, had escaped the long

talons of a mink-eating raptor. He was tired and in all likelihood, lost. He remembered Mooch challenging his male mink-hood that first night, the night this all began and how helpless he had felt throughout that ordeal. His inescapable blindness sheathed him in darkness with no glimmer of light, but providence... fate, whatever you wanted to call it, had beckoned him to this moment and he had no choice but to follow. He gathered his wits and some courage and moved on....

***

"Rise and shine my little stinky heads." Farmer Tucci placed his grub-filled bucket on the floor. He looked around at all the wide-eyed minks looking back at him. "Hey little my little bambinos, everybody early risers today? Waiting for your food are we?"

He walked down the row and scooped rabbit, ground and forever cold, and sang a song. "I like to sing... *Ol sola mi, Ol sola you...* but my wife always tells me to *shutta yo face*. I'd like to tell her to *shutta yo mouth*. ...That mouth of hers never stops. Always busting my chops and breaking my bones about something. *Guiseppe, I need a new car. Guiseppe, we need a new TV. Guiseppe look at these new shoes aren't they adorable, I got them in five colors* ...Like she doesn't have enough shoes. What is it with women and their shoes? How many feet does a woman really have that she needs all those shoes?"

He shoved more rabbit slop into the push-in trays. "Oh,

and let's not forget the hair and nails. Gimmy a break! *...I need money to get my hair done."* Tucci mimicked. *"Look at my nails. I'm tired of cleaning the house. We make enough money to hire someone to clean this house. Why should I do it? You have hired help on the farm, so why shouldn't I? Look at what it's doing to my nails. It isn't fair!"*

He stood in front of Mooch's pen. Every eye was focused on him as he pulled back the tray, shoveled out a mound and shoved it back in. He started to turn when he suddenly stopped. Turning slowly around, he bent over with his big moon face, to study the inside. Mooch could feel his stare riveted on him and looked away several times afraid to meet his glare.

"What in carnation happened in there?" He twisted around to look into the cage from the back. "Where's the other one?" It was then that he noticed piles of fur scattered all around the floor of the cage. His face suddenly grew dark red, while his eyes narrowed. "Don't I give you enough to eat?" He exploded. "You bloated overindulgent pig? Bones and all? I never saw anything like this before! You ate my best pelt you over-bloated cannibal! Do you realize how much money that one mink you ate was worth to me? . You're going to pay for this. I swear you are going to PAY!!"

Mooch cowered away from the face, as anger and spit from Tucci's mouth showered him.

"That's it. I should have gotten rid of you the moment I saw you. That's what I get for being a nice guy! Thought I could use you for something. What was I thinking? You are scrap!!!

Hear me SCRAP!!!!"

Tucci grabbed Mooch's cage, hoisted it roughly into the air and slammed it down on the floor. Mooch bounced off the top. Every one of his fellow minks started to yell and scream at once, especially Edna who grabbed at the mesh and screamed above the rest.

"Put that cage back you evil over grown ox!" Tucci could hear their nervous hissing, squealing and snarling but ignored them.

Tucci shook the cage. "You worm-wooded blimp! Your days are numbered you mutant tub of lard. You like to eat do you? Well you'll never get one more morsel of food from me. Die of starvation for all I care. Your roommate was your last meal"

He started toward the door. Mooch's entire body cringed as he looked back at all his new friends who were yelling for him to hang in there and not to worry that everything was going to be alright. He clutched onto the mesh as he was swung back and forth in his cage. He could feel his glands starting to release, but he held on, promising himself that for once, he was going to control this, that he was master over his body, and not the other way around. He thought of Zeto out there. How brave he had been. *"Tell Zeto I didn't release,"* he yelled as the doors of the shed slammed closed.

...The Grand General was becoming frustrated. The maps they had requested were delayed because they were classified. Who ever heard of *human maps* being classified? He supposed they were difficult to obtain, but he was looking at eight days now, and he knew the longer the wait, the colder the trail.

He was the Defense Minister and Grand General of the entire Royal Military and he had seen many human maps. How was he suppose to do his job without them? The courtiers were doing what they could. Only a sovereign could obtain such documentation. Prince Montega promised that he would have what he needed by tomorrow at the latest and then surprised the General by giving him carte blanche over the necessary steps to take in order to retrieve Count Ulderico.

He looked over at Colonel Lugasteino trying to decide which direction to tell him to head. He had never felt so helpless. Ulderico Palace had been set up as a command post. He practically lived here. The Contessa was counting on him and he could not let her down, not to mention her son.

"Colonel Lugasteino, I would like you to take twenty of soldiers and follow the road that you and your men found the first day here. Move ten in one direction and ten in the other direction. These roads lead to Guiseppe Tucci's Mink Farm which is somewhere not far from here. I can feel it in my bones. With or without a human map, I would rather be doing something, than just sitting around waiting and doing nothing."

"If we find the farm, sir, are we to take action?" Lugasteino asked.

"No. Leave five men posted and report back to me so that we can investigate further. I need maps. We will call in all reinforcements first. The rule of our species has been to stay out of human realms, but that is changing. We have watched our kind dwindle and our species endangered over the decades because of these farms with no end in sight.

Now that Prince Montega has taken the helm, his modern, more liberal thinking is changing the way we view and react to the human world. He has made a decision to move into their domain and we will start as soon as I have those satellite maps and have come up with a strategy. Total annihilation of this particular farm is imminent."

"Yes sir." Colonel Lugasteino saluted and made his way toward his unit.

***

Zeto traveled much better during the day. He followed close to the road. He had no idea how many kilometers that he had gone. It was near dusk, on the ninth day. He had been on the run for forty-eight hours and he was still alive....

He took one catnap inside and old abandoned muskrat den that smelled so bad he didn't think he would be able to stay there at first. But he needed the shelter and the sleep, even a wink. He could feel his strength weakening. He also needed to eat. He knew his blood sugar was low, but no way was he about to kill something to satisfy his hunger. This was one trait of his nature he chose to ignore.

He walked a little further when he heard the sound of water

coming from somewhere nearby. He needed water. He was so thirsty. He walked in the direction of the lapping water sound. It grew louder and more distinct. He stood before an open brook and hunkered down to quench his thirst. He drank and drank and when he finished he splashed water all over his face. Feeling refreshed, he sat on the bank of the rivulet and contemplated his next move. His stomach screamed out for food. Sharp pains of hunger cramped him. He looked down and saw a big fat juicy worm or some night crawler.

No, he couldn't. They were very tasty fried and dipped into Chipotle sauce, but alive and raw... never. He sat a little longer, deciding to head back toward the road. He looked down at the worm again and before he could stop himself, he pounced on it and swallowed it whole. *"What was he turning into?"* He thought to himself. *An animal?*

He retraced his steps and walked with a little more spunk, noticing that darkness crept in without him noticing. His stomached churned, either from hunger or from a live worm crawling around inside of him. He couldn't decide which. He shook his head when he picked up the scent of something. He sniffed the air again and still the scent.

He crouched down in the tall dead grass and tried to decipher the smell. It smelled like one of his own, but because he didn't trust his instincts, decided to find a hollow cavity somewhere and hide. Before he could move, he could hear grass rustling just ahead. He froze. The fur covering his body stood on edge. He knew it could not end this way. He had come so far. *Please, not now.*

What was it? A fox? He scanned the grass when he heard a faint rustling again. He had never fought off anything, but he was preparing himself to fight to the death if need be. He sniffed again. The smell was familiar. Smelled like one of his own... he was sure of it.

"Who is out there?" He yelled. The grass moved in front of him and what he saw almost made him faint away. A mink stood before him. A large strapping mink wearing military stripes and a beret'.

This mink was followed by nine others soldiers clad in black from head to toe. He had never seen such uniforms in his life.

"I am Colonel Lugasteino from a branch of the Royal Mink Intelligence Agency. I am pleased to meet you Count Ulderico. We have been searching for you for many days. We picked up your scent about ten minutes ago."

"You must come with me." Zeto said desperately. "They need help. They are back there in cages waiting to meet their deaths. You must come with me immediately."

"All due respect to you Count, but there are only ten of us at this post. My orders are to return to the Grand General at Ulderico Palace. No action until further ordered."

"No. I demand that you follow me at once. My orders take precedence."

"I am sorry Sire, but your orders are overridden by my

General's, Tito DiNicolantinio. I am only following orders."

"I will not go back with you. I need to get them out of Shed #1. We are wasting time."

"Please sir, follow us back or we will have to take you back by force. I am sorry Count Ulderico, but I have my orders to follow. Let the General decide."

"Well, I refuse to be bullied. I will not go with you."

The five soldiers, thinking with one mind, under the specific orders of their Grand General, grabbed Zeto and in a matter of seconds had him handcuffed to the Colonel's wrist.

"I am sorry Count Ulderico that it had to come to this but I...."

"I know, don't tell me," Zeto looked down at the cuffs, "You have your orders."

***

...The next few days were frightful. Adrianna bit her bottom lip and looked down at her niece. She could not remember a millisecond in her life when she was this afraid. It had been two days. Two days of pacing and wondering and worrying. Her mind conjured horrific images of Zeto's demise, beginning when he stepped through the tunnel aperature.

And poor Mooch. What of him? No one had seen or even picked up his scent from the morning Tucci had carried him through the door of their shed. They all felt responsible and helpless. No one couldn't understand his last remark... something about telling Zeto he didn't release. They all had discussed it many times and they came up empty.

Inside, her brain was screaming. Beppe decided that Frank and Dominic would leave together if nothing happened by tomorrow night. She held her breath. He had promised her that he would come back and she knew that if he *could*... he would.

Chapter Nine

Back Home

"Z*EEETO!!!*" Contessa Arabella hurried from the staircase as she turned and watched her son walk through the front doors....

She scurried down the steps clutching the handrail and ran toward him as he stood in the entranceway. She grabbed him, held him in her arms, sobbing while stroking his head and neck. Zeto wrapped his one arm around her. The other was attached to Colonel Lugasteino. "Oh Zeto, my son, Oh praise be...."

"Mama." He breathed hard trying to hold back a medley of emotions that sprang to the surface at seeing her again. For a time, he thought he never would. Feeling her shaking body in his arms, Zeto clung to her tighter. Looking over her shoulder, he met Uncle Angelo's warm eyes, standing with another mink he had never seen before.

"Uncle Angelo," Zeto called to him, reaching out with his free arm. He watched as he hurried over to them and wrapped his long fore arms around both his sister and his nephew. They stood there for several minutes saying nothing.

"Nephew," Uncle Angelo took a step back wiping at a small tear. "You have given us quite a scare. Leaving without security. Whoever heard of such a thing? What I should do is turn you over my knee and spank your bottom back-end for scaring us like that. You know, you're never too old."

Zeto smiled over his mother's shoulder and then looked down at her. "Mother. Look at me."

The Contessa's wet face looked up at her son. She placed both of her paws on either side of his face. "Zeto, my sweet, I have been so lost without you. I died a little with each day of not knowing where you were."

It was then she noticed that he was holding her with only one arm. She turned and followed his other stretched fore arm over to where it connected with Colonel Lugasteino's. "What is the meaning of this?"

Her gaze went from the Colonel to the Grand General. "Tito, please tell me why my son is handcuffed to your Colonel?"

The mink was a stranger to Zeto. He watched as he walked toward them.

"Zeto, this is the Grand General, Tito DiNicolantonio, an old friend of my family. These are all his men." She looked back over at the Grand General. "Tito, why is my son handcuffed like a common criminal?"

The Grand General reached out and shook Zeto's extended paw. Never looking at his Colonel, the Grand General said, "He was handcuffed because he resisted our escort back I suppose. My orders were explicit and implicitly followed. Do not blame Colonel Lugasteino. Blame me. They were my orders."

"But Tito, why did you order handcuffing?" Wet tears hung in her eyes as she looked into his. "I do not understand."

"Apparently, your son was not of the same mind to be

escorted back here. His plans were obviously adverse to my plar
They all turned and looked at Zeto.

He looked over at the Colonel. "First, unlock these."

The Colonel retrieved a key from his jacket pocket anc
unlocked the cuffs.

Zeto rubbed his wrist and turned and faced a group of
puzzled faces, among them, several soldiers and some of the
household staff.

"He cuffed me because I wanted them to come with me,
back to that death camp where for the last week. I have been stuffed
into a cage that was so small and shallow I could not stand, left in
freezing temperatures for three-hour periods so that my fur will
grow thicker. All this for the sole purpose that I could be skinned
and my pelt then sold for money when it was thick enough. I was
forced to eat cold ground –and in all probability, diseased rabbit
morning and night, existed in perpetual darkness and had to listen to
a *demente'* ridicule and mock us daily, and it is my *duty* to get the
rest out."

"Mother… I must go back. There are so many. While we
are standing here in this sweet reunion, our own kind will be
electrocuted, gassed, sprayed or injected with poisonous
insecticides. Thousands will die unless we do something.

How can any of us stand by and allow the extermination of
our own kind and do nothing! Mooch is back there. …And mama,"
he looked deep into maternal eyes. "My future, my life, my destiny
is trapped in a cage with her niece back there. I promised her, I

.." of them, that I would come back for them and if I have

or with just my own personal arsenal of minks, then I

He turned back to the rest of them. "I have already wasted time wondering around in the woods, following a road that I sure to remember. That was three days ago!"

He looked over at the Grand General. "I need your help. ..se. I need somebody to help me. Your soldiers with mine, but .. must go, *pronto militare!*"

For the first time Contessa Arabella noticed his dishevelment, his matted fur, dirty, full of burrs, and the fetid smell he was drenched in. His clothes were torn and raggedy. "My son," the Contessa took a step back. "You escaped and were the only one who was to bring them freedom?"

She could not fully comprehend what he was saying. "You were alone in the woods for two days and nights all alone? Is that what you are saying?"

"Almost three." Zeto could feel a panic rising. "And we are wasting more time." Why were they all just standing there looking at him? Why weren't they moving?

"But you have no night vision, my son. No scenting or hunting abilities. How can this be?"

He looked down at his mother noticing that she had lost weight and exhaustion had taken over most of her beauty. Tired eyes, eyes that hadn't slept. Circles of faint darkness shaded under them. Deep lines etched around the corners of her mouth. He felt a pang slice through him for causing her anguish.

"Colonel Lugasteino," she addressed him formally, "You did not rescue my son from that... that place?"

"No, Contessa." The Colonel took a step further into the room. "Your son was found less than a kilometer away from his last scented location. We did not rescue him. We scented him at 200 meters from what was our location at the time."

Her astonishment animated her face. "My son, how has this happened? You broke out of this mink farm and traveled with night blindness for three days and nights and found your way back?"

Zeto took a deep breath and walked further into the entrance hall. "I made it back to where Mooch and I were trapped. But please, all of you..."

His eyes scanned the room as he turned and met every one's gaze. "We have no time." We need to hurry and...."

He began to feel himself sway, but he continued to walk. "We must leave immediately." A blast of dizziness caught him off guard; its suddenness caused him to stumble. Uncle Angelo and the Grand General grabbed him under both fore arms before he could sink to the floor.

Contessa Arabella shouted for them to take him to his study and lay him down on the sofa.

"Jed," she yelled for the only weasel on her staff. He was standing to the side, slightly smiling as though the display before him had somehow entertained him.

Against her better judgment, she had taken him in after he

had been nearly beaten to death after trying to chisel a shopkeeper out of some money. She gave him a chance to make an *honest* living, but he still made her nervous. She decided days ago that he would have to go. Watching him now only reinforced her resolve. "Please tell cook that we need chicken broth. Immediately."

Jed smiled at her and started toward the kitchen, taking his good old time.

They carried Zeto to his study. They placed him onto an overstuffed leather couch next to a roaring fire. He tried to shake the wooziness, but it would not abate, it intensified in fact. He shook his head trying to clear the fuzziness that gripped him.

"Zeto," he heard his mother say, but she sounded as though she was speaking from so far away. He strained to hear her. "You need to eat something. You cannot go back to that horrid place."

"I… have to get… her…Adrianna… have to see…." He tried to stand to fight their fore paws grabbing at him, all of them pushing him back down and he felt himself slipping, and a grogginess so strong had vanquished his ability to move. He closed his eyes and slumped down while blackness engulfed him.

"Zeto." Contessa sat next to her slumped over son. She pulled him into her arms and held him, stroking his cheek and whispering into his ear. "Sleep my son. Just sleep."

She looked up at her brother. "Angelo, call for Doctor Anzio immediately."

Angelo nodded and hurried out of the room. Tito bent down on the floor in front of her watching as she gently kissed her son, telling him over and over that she loved him.

"He is fine. Just suffering from exposure and exhaustion. He needs to rest a while and make sure you get some light foods and fluids into him. I am going. We have never involved our military in the human realm, but tonight, I must gather as many minks, weasels, badgers, polecats, all of your minks, and your brother Angelo's troops.

I have also sent for reinforcements that are due later this evening. By dawn, I plan to march to this farm. I will not rest until every mink, young, old, male, female, and every child mink are free of that place. No building will be left standing and your son would never forgive me, or you if he were not there. But tonight he needs to rest. He needs to sleep. He will wake up soon. When he does, I want you to come for me. Your son and I need to have a little heart-to-heart."

"How can you understand him so well Tito? In many ways he reminds me a lot of you when you were a young officer. You were also bullheaded." She smiled into his face never stopping her light stoking of Zeto's ears.

"Not me Lady Arabell but Salvo. It was Salvo that was always the bullhead."

"Well, I always thought the two of you were very much alike, even way back then. She smiled over at him. "Both of you cut from the same cloth… same temperament. You were both also extremely competitive, and let's not forget arrogant at times, strong-willed… bullheaded. And you both were wonderful. Both of you,

-so, so wonderful. Zeto is very idealistic like the two of you use to be until cynicism set in with old age. But you must promise me Tito that Zeto be kept away from any dangers that may present themselves."

"You have my word Arabell." The Grand General stood and started to make his way out of the room when he heard her say as he opened the door....

"And when this is all over, you must stay and feast with us; after all it isn't every day that a son returns home to his mama telling her that he has found true love."

He nodded and smiled. The Grand General closed the door quietly and went in search of Colonel Lugasteino. They needed to assemble the troops.

***

It had been three days...and Adrianna felt herself losing control, losing her grip. Adrianna bit her bottom lip and looked down at her niece. Three whole days, seventy-two hours of waiting, vigilant and obsessing on his traveling in deep dark unfriendly woodlands without ever having been in a position to fight or flee, or to feed himself. Three days. Was this a bad sign? She would never understand why they had allowed him to go?

Beppe and the rest made a decision that they would give him twelve more hours, and if he hadn't returned with his army as promised, they would send Dominic and Frank. A few even intimated that maybe he was not coming back, that he might have changed his mind once he reached home or was rescued, deciding not to involve himself any further in this matter, and this angered her. She stood firm and told the rest of the group that if he could get back to them, that he would, that he had *promised.* Only his death would keep him away, this she knew. How dare they think that he would just forget about them and go on with his life as though nothing had ever happened. She never doubted him for a moment. She closed her eyes; an overwhelming cluster of emotions seized her as she tried to avert ugly pictures of him out there being viciously cornered and taken. She turned in her tiny-wired confinement, and swooped her niece into her arms. Zeto would come back. God would not do this to her. She clutched Marcellina in her arms and rocked her back and forth. She had just found him. He would come back. He *had* to come back. He had promised.

.... Zeto woke with a sudden jolt. He sat up straight and looked over at the clock on the mantle. How long had he been out? He glanced over at the long arched windows on either side of the fireplace and could see that it was still dark outside. He wiped his paws over his face. He slowly rose from the couch when a sound from behind him caused him to spin around.

The Grand General stood from behind Zeto's polished mahogany desk and walked around and leaned on the edge. A small desk lamp burned over what looked to him like a very large human satellite map. "Did you have a nice cat nap Count Ulderico?"

Zeto could feel a headache niggling at both temples. "I feel like I've been hit by a train if you really want to know. How long have I been out and how long have you been sitting over there? I have to get out of here. I can't believe you let me sleep this long...."

The General was staring down at the map. "I have been here for a little over an hour restudying this map." You needed the sleep. Your experience caught up with you. Your mother sent for some Azio fellow, a doctor, to examine you. The diagnosis was exhaustion and exposure, as I surmised.

If you hadn't slept, you would be useless to every mink that is counting on you. You're not a trained soldier. You have been in the woods for almost three days without sleep or food. What I would do if I were you is take a nice long hot shower and eat something light. We leave at dawn.

It will take hours to reach this farm and we move at a reasonably rapid pace. It is a long march and you need to be ready for it. So, you needed the rest, and now you need the nourishment to get your energy level up. We will not reach our destination until well after dark tomorrow. I have assembled quite a mishmash of ready and able soldiers.

Go clean yourself up. Eat something light, nothing heavy, drink lots of water. Remember, no matter how anxious you are, and I realize you are very anxious to get back, that we must do this the right way if we are to free so many. I will be in command and you will follow *my* orders Count. I hope that is understood. We leave

Castello di Ulderico at first light."

"I understand." Zeto said slowly walking toward the General. He leaned his head to the right. "Let me ask you something General. Why are you doing all this? I mean, why are you involving yourself? I realize the ties my family has with H.R.H. Prince Montega, but regardless, someone of your esteemed rank and level never gets their paws dirty, none of you ever get near enough to the real action. I don't understand your presence here and or your involvement."

"Let's just say that I am doing this for old friends. I was well acquainted with both your mother and father way back when. I won't tell you how *far* …way back when." He shook his head and smiled. "We were all very young. You know, you're a great deal like your father."

"I hope that's a good thing." Zeto rubbed his eyes. He spotted a pair of his reading glasses sitting among the clutter on his desk. Funny that he hadn't thought about them.

"Yes, it is a good thing." Zeto watched as he spoke; his whiskers were as white as the fur on the sides of his face. His face was long and thin, his jowls were beginning to sag, but he was statuesque, his shoulders still broad, and waist trim and every part of him exuded power.

"Your father was a very unique mink. When I first saw you walk through the door this morning, it was like traveling through time. The resemblance, uncanny."

The Grand General stopped and motioned for Zeto to sit

down on a chair in the front of his desk. "Your father also often acted on impulse before thinking things through," he said as he raised one brow, "so at least you come by it honestly. You were about to go back to that farm when my Colonel found you, without the provisions needed, to do what I have been painstakingly planning this entire week. You would have ruined all my planning, and more than likely gotten yourself killed in the process. So it is very important, Count, and I cannot emphasize this enough, which is to allow me to do what I have come here to do. This mink farm is a fortress that has never been breached before. We are about to engage humans for the very first time in our history, and this undertaking must go according to *my* plans... *my* orders, and if something goes wrong, it will be *my* neck....

Now that we have that out of the way, let me answer the next part of your question... why am I getting my paws dirty? Let's just say that I could have sent another commander to do this job for me, but as I said before, I was well acquainted with your parents. I understand your mother's emotional gauge, and with losing a husband after all those years of marriage not so long ago, I decided that I had to be a physical presence here. We are old friends and I knew that she would trust me and I suppose my calendar was free. I was out of the country when your father died and I have to say that this world is a little darker without him."

He turned back to the map. "Now, I want you to go clean yourself up, eat light and drink as much as you can and listen very carefully... when you have finished, you and I must sit down and go over this map. I have studied it and briefed all my officers, but I need to know exactly where everything is located on this farm, anything that I may have overlooked, as much as you can possibly recall... the type of locks on the sheds, types and styles of cages and the locks on them and so on and so forth. We have a few hours before daybreak."

Zeto understood how some minks were elevated into lofty posts and positions. Tito DiNicolantonio was known as a great *comandare*, a legend actually, and he was discovering he was also a first-rate mink.

"I will do as you say, but I have one request, really two. First, I would like to free all the minks that are in shed #1. They are personal friends and there is a female mink in there that I need to make sure is taken to safety. She has been in one of those puny cages with her niece for close to eighteen days. I don't want her to be frightened. I want to go into that shed with your soldiers and be there for her. She needs to be protected when this chaos starts."

"There will be no chaos, sire. I do not work that way. I am a perfectionist. I am precise and methodical so that there are very few surprises thrown at me, ever. I hate surprises of that nature and I rarely encounter them. You may free your female."

Zeto smiled at the older mink leaning half on and half off his desk. "I will go then to the second request. The second request is that you let me have five minutes alone with Guisseppe Tucci. Your soldiers can be present, but there is something I have to get off my chest and I am sure I will never get another opportunity."

209

"That is doable. Only five?" He grinned.

"That depends upon Tucci. It may require more." He smiled over at the General and for the first time in ten days, a calmness settled over him, like everything was going to turn out all right. "And on that note, General, I bid you adieu."

The General smiled once the Count closed the doors behind him. He liked him. He shook his head and smiled again. Salvo must have derived a great sense of pride in him. He turned and walked around to the back of the desk and sat down. There was much to extrapolate from this map and time was growing short.

The Count of Ulderico and the Grand General opened the front doors leading out of *Palazzo del Ulderico* at four-thirty AM and walked out onto its expanded portico. Zeto was struck mute as he looked out over an ocean flow of uniforms. Brown, tan, blue and gray, red stripes, gold stripes, green stripes and berets covering the heads of soldiers that were literally spread over kilometers of land.

Wolverines, Polecats, badgers, regiments and regiments of minks covered his land as far as the eye could see. He had never seen such a spectacle. They stood by the thousands, silent and at attention waiting for the Grand General to address them. All higher-ranking Senior Officers stood at least ten meters in front of their units.

The General stood on the top step and in a booming, masterly assertive voice and with aid of a microphone said:

"Your commanding officers have briefed you all on the

intricacies of this assignment. These soldiers that you see clad in black behind Colonel Lugasteino are my tactical units called COBRA, an elite group that HRH Prince Montaga and myself created. They have been brought in as tactical and scent specialists. They will seal off the farmhouse. This job is essentially our first strike and that is to subdue our friend Signor Tucci and any other human found on this farm. The COBRAS will then aid the other units with whatever needs to be done to accomplish our goal as quickly as possible. My COBRAS' are all officers. They are to be given the respect one would give a superior officer. They will remain anonymous. Only Senior Officer, Colonel Lugasteino and myself know their identies.

Wolverines... your jobs are to seal off the property perimeters, making sure Tucci and his wife do not escape and also, once the harvested minks start running, you will be there to aid them.

Polecats, your jobs are to free every mink from sheds one through eight. Your Commanding Officer has already briefed you on locks, on both the shed and cage doors. Get them out and take them into the woods. Count Ulderico, will be accompanying you on this mission.

Minks and Badgers, on the north face, you will find enormous barrack-like barns filled with approximately 25,000 minks. There are two such structures. Your job is the most difficult and will take the longest. Release them all from their cages. Scatter them into the forest. They need to know that they are now expected to hunt for themselves. Hopefully Mother Nature will kick in. For those that are young and alone, let them know of the few existing resources that address our youth on hunting and scenting procurement.

Remember. This is a non-violent strike. I am your General and each and every one of you is a reflection of me. Make me proud. What makes our races unique from that of the humans is that we seldom accomplish our goals, interests or conflicts with the use of violence. All of you are doing what is important, and I look up to each an every one of you soldiers here today because you represent the good of our world, the watchers and the keepers of peace and freedom."

He paused for a moment to gather his thoughts. "You are all heroes in my book, because you are taking action against a wrong. That's what heroes do. They change what is wrong and bad and make it right and good. We wear uniforms that separate us from civilians. These uniforms tell a story about each and every one of you. These uniforms tell the world that you are busy at your job of making our world safe because you protect it and if need be, you are willing give up your lives to safeguard that freedom in which we were all born to own.

With that being said. Let's do it soldiers! *Dissss...missed!"*

An ear-splitting ovation sounded across the masses of assembled soldiers. Zeto could feel chills climbing up over his fore arms and neck. He had never seen or heard anything like this It was surreal. The fur on the back of his neck and back stood on end.

He and the General descended the steps and with pride. Even though Zeto's title out-ranked the General's, he walked slightly behind him as an opening parted for them, as the soldiers screamed and moved to the side to let him pass. Zeto looked at their faces as they made their way through the masses, and to his astonishment, what was written there blew him out of the water. Not only was hero-worship written there, but *love.* They all loved this mink. He watched the general make his way ahead of him, through a path of flailing arms, which he stopped on occasion to embrace paws or to pat a shoulder. Singularly, this General, had not only gathered their respect and admiration, but he had down right captured their love.

As the human race, Americans especially, worshiped rock stars, sports stars and actors; these soldiers looked up at him with the passion of a thousand screaming fans. The General was right, this was what was important. These were the types of minks he wanted his offspring to worship and look up to and emulate.

Leadership and acts of courage should be what the media focused upon and recognized those that made the world freer, those that made a difference, those that stood up and put their lives on the line to keep us all safe. Zeto believed that this was the highest compliment anyone could bestow upon another mink, and that was to revere them, and personalize them.

He looked over his shoulder at a long line of Senior

Officers that followed their General with dignity and pride, proud to be following behind such an acclaimed and noble mink. To him, each one of these mink soldiers was a hero. They all deserved his respect. He had gained respect and admiration only through his born position and titles, not because of anything he had accomplished or done for his fellow mink. That would change. He had changed. He would do things to make *that* difference count. Isn't that what it was all about? All of them, each and every soldier had come together this morning, united for one common goal, and that goal was freedom, a freedom he had taken for granted, until it was gone.

Zeto hoped Tucci had fallen for the farce of Mooch eating him and had not retaliated by opening every pen and sifting through until he found the hole at the bottom of Venanzio's cage. The thought, and the number of times it would spring into his mind, bothered him. It made the inside of him shutter. He and the General had talked at length about how the minks in his shed had combined their skills and efforts to break out, how they had worked during the nights while Tucci slept. Why it made the most sense that he try to return since it was his scent that was being searched for.

The General reassured him that when they reached Tucci's Mink Farm that they would more than likely discover that he had not tried to double up on guarding or protecting it. That Tucci did not have the fortitude or the mental prowess to do so.

The General had narrowed his eyes as they pierced through Zeto's and said, "I am certain that Signore Tucci could see with his own eyes the hole that was chewed through the cage and the tunnel dug under the shed and never believe for one second that it had been the work of the very minks he had locked in his cages. He would blame it on rats or other predators, but never that his minks had the intelligence, nor the withstanding to pull it off. He would never let himself believe it.

We don't exist to him Zeto, as walking, breathing, intelligent beings with our own lives to lead. We are pelts, fur for money. When we reach Tucci's Farm, I predict that it will be no more secured than what is his usual practice. But, just in case, I am prepared for both."

Zeto prayed that all of them were safe and were where he had left them. He could not bear the thought of Adrianna being stuck in that little cage with her young niece, waiting, as the hours ticked by for him to return. He wondered if she thought something had happened to him and that their fate was sealed. His heart picked up some speed, if that were possible after what he had just witnessed. He wondered if she was okay. After this was over tonight, he looked forward to a little alone time with Signor Tucci, which would mark a new but improved beginning for Zeto Pantaleone Ulderico, the male adult mink... not the Count. He would come down to Tucci's level of thinking and thinking about what was to come enervated him to move faster, to push himself harder. His adrenalin flowed at a steady but rapid speed. Alone with Tucci. This human had no idea what waited for him.

Chapter Ten

The Invasion

I t was past eight when they reached Tucci's Mink Farm. It had taken fifteen hours to cover an eight-mile radius of ground. They shaved two hours off their approximated time of arrival by crossing an extended arm of the Tiber River that winded through the forest. The two hours saved were spent in two one-hour breaks.

...The General looked over at Zeto and said in a voice barely audible to anyone else.... "Our route courses through the Tiber. Do you think you can handle this channel? Swimming may come natural, it may not, but we must shorten our journey. My soldiers need to stop and rest, rejuvenate, recharge their batteries, eat and drink something and this route will allow for that. Will you be alright?"

There followed a pause. Zeto took a deep breath. Did he have a choice? "I will attempt it."

The General smiled over at him. "I do believe Count that had you gone into the military instead of your current role you would have one day made an excellent soldier. You do have all the markings of one, but I will be right next to you to make sure that you don't drown. Your mother would never forgive me."

Zeto found the idea repugnant. "I think I would rather drown than for any of your soldiers to witness my utter and complete humiliation at never learning how to swim."

The General chuckled at this. "I can be very discreet."

"N... No thank you." Zeto stammered. "I'd prefer drowning."

***

Rows of massive trees lined the river's edge, stripped bare and naked, allowing weak rays of dim light to trickle through their twisted branches. With the General still beside him, Zeto clenched his jaw as they approached the lapping water along the bank. His eyes closed and he winced as he calculated the distance across. *No easy feat for an experienced swimmer.* He said a short prayer.

The General turned, his eyes zeroing in on Zeto's and said, "It looks a lot harder than it is." He smiled again and whispered. "There is only one thing to say in an instance like this son, and that is: *...sink or swim....*"

Zeto walked into a blast of freezing water; so frigid it took his breath away. He didn't have time to think or to concentrate on what he was supposed to be doing. The water was far too frigid to allow any fear to creep into his bones about the act of swimming and as though his body had done it a hundred times before, he simply, began to swim. His body began to function as though it had a mind of its own. He had always wondered what swimming would feel like, the buoyancy of gliding over top of water or slicing through it. He had seen it done, but it had never appealed to him enough to learn how.

It was an exhilaration he never expected. He moved across it feeling a sense of weightlessness, of being picked up and carried. It must be inbred, because here he was, moving over water, keeping up with the General, and seeing that all his Senior Officers and soldiers were crossing behind them. When they reached the other side, he thought of the night he and Mooch stood on a very similar bank and how Mooch had refused to even consider swimming across. Why was it that he could do it on his first attempt and Mooch had tried several times and failed? *What was different?*

Maybe he could do it because there was no other option open to him. Maybe he had gained confidence that his natural abilities would take over as they had with all the other physical elements in his make-up. Maybe he knew that this water route would bring him closer to Adrianna and that a minute wasted was a minute longer that she would be confined in that cage. *A lot of maybes.* Again he thought of providence.

....The General and Zeto stood on frozen pine needles in front of Tucci's Mink Farm. They concealed themselves under a canopy of evergreens and squatty bushes. Mud smeared his face, leaves still clung to still damp trousers and a thick jacket, but Zeto felt nothing but the flip-flopping of his stomach. It all looked the same, although he had never seen it at night from this perspective, it looked as it did the night he had fled. He could remember only bits and pieces of that night, but one thing he remembered clearly was the small red sheds. *All eight of them.* He had been very busy that night memorizing the road leading out, so he could recall it when he came back in. All of it was the same as he left it. From here he could see Tucci's sprawling log cabin style home in the distance. But his eyes stayed riveted on *Shed #1.*

"A one story ranch. That makes this easier. No upper floors to contend with. The blue prints of the house were not available. We didn't know the layout. This is a welcome surprise. Colonel Lugasteino," the General called.

"Sir," he answered.

"Get your men ready to seal off the house. I want Tucci and his wife bound and brought outside. Leave them in front of the house. I want both of them to witness what our species and our cousin species can do."

"Yes Sir." Colonel Lugasteino saluted, turned and walked back to the line.

Minutes later Zeto could see the COBRA unit's stealth led by Lugasteino, as they soundlessly approached and surrounded the house. Heavy ropes hung around their necks; some paired up and dragged them. The COBRA soldiers where garbed totally in black from head to toe, so they were enveloped in the night's darkness which made it difficult for Zeto to see from such a distance where the night ended and the soldier's bodies began. He could see some movement here and there, but nothing distinct and he supposed that this was the way they wanted it, the way they planned all their attack and rescue procedures.

An eerie silence hung over the farm. Zeto's whole body felt stiff, tension-filled. *Could they be scented?* He whispered to the General, "Can the COBRA soldiers be scented by the minks occupying this farm?

The General replied in a very matter-of-fact whisper, never taking his eyes from his binoculars, "No. Their scent sacs have been removed. Once removed and with intense training regiments, they have become a world-renowned scent specialist team. They cannot be scented or tracked by any species including man. But I am sure *our* scents have been picked up. There are so many minks housed here however, I don't think they can distinguish ours as new scents."

...Suddenly a loud crash of breaking glass disturbed the night's solitude. Zeto jerked around and watched as COBRA soldiers climbed through smashed in windows and broken down doors. Ear piercing shrieks shattered throughout the ranch house, a human woman and man yelling and screaming words he couldn't quite comprehend from where he stood. Minutes later, thirty or more COBRA soldiers dragged a woman down the front steps and released her once they reached the ground.

She was twisting and scrambling in her binding, yelling in frustration while trying to kick out at them and turn her body over in an effort to stand. The mink specialists ignored her, bound her mouth shut with duct tape and went back into the house.

221

A few moments later, a hog-tied Signore Tucci was dragged roughly down steps by all seventy-five soldiers. Extremely overweight, screaming bloody murder, and dressed in bright red long johns, Tucci was thrown on the cold ground. They taped his mouth shut. He lay on his stomach squirming on the frozen earth where he was thrown, flopping around like a giant fish. How they ever managed to bind his wrists to his ankles behind his back would always remain a mystery to Zeto.

The unit stood unmoving, waiting for the next regiment to follow. Quietness once again fell upon the farm.

Senior Officer Biorg led the next strike. They all watched from the edge of the forest, as the General sent the Wolverine unit to seal off the farm's perimeter. Zeto stood silent as he watched them form one single file line and make their way around the farm, moving in alternating opposite directions. The Wolverines, uniform-clad, had been brought to Italy from the Scandinavia Peninsula. They enjoyed arctic temperature and were known for their sometimes-explosive behavior and bad language. However, these soldiers were well trained and predictable and only used that part of their nature as a last resort. Wolverines were able to bring down animals as large as a moose. They were brave, fearless and loyal to a fault... the essential ingredients needed for excellent soldiers.

The Grand General had worked with these soldiers before on two other missions, and he was assured of their dedication and allegiance. They were an interesting species, well-muscled and fearless, but with a sense of humor, always good for a good practical joke or prank. Wolverines were rarely serious about anything but when they were called to arms, the soldier in them would kick in and everything would change. Their rigorous training as a ground unit and unending energy qualified them as some of the best soldiers in the world. If he were to go onto a battlefield, the General conclude, he would want a Wolverine spotting his back.

Once he was satisfied with their positions, the General looked over at Zeto. He was ready to send the European polecats to the sheds. Polecats also made fine soldiers, however they tended to be a more serious group. Their uniforms were dark olive with a deep scarlet trim, and solid red berets. Zeto flinched as they formed a line behind him.

The General nodded at Senior Officer Ballisto and said, "Not one beam standing."

Senior Officer Ballisto nodded and looked over at Zeto. "Sir, when you are ready."

Zeto had no idea he would be leading this attack. He turned back toward the eight sheds. His breath came in stinging waves. She was there. He knew Shed #1 would be first. He started toward it with more than three hundred polecat soldiers following behind....

With their noses pressed against metal wire, every one of them inside Shed #1 stood as best they could. They were rattled awake from loud human screaming that was cut off as quickly as it had started. They were all sure that the screams came from Signor Tucci and his wife. They also heard mumbled voices, scrambling feet and a conglomeration of new scents from various animals that seemed to be all part of the weasel family. And then everything grew still and very quiet.

"They're here!" Beppe bowed his head and fell to his knees and appeared to be in silent prayer.

Venanzio looked toward the door of the shed. "I knew the Count would come back. He wasn't going to let us rot here. Like zero doubt man."

Frank looked at the group as a whole, and felt his heart thumping. They were all pressed against their cage walls staring at the shed door. "And just in time Dominic…just in time."

Adrianna grabbed her niece. "I told you he would come back… I told all of you. He promised us." She squeezed Marcellina tighter. Tears glistened and then descended down her cheeks. Her heart was bursting, thumping like the feet of a thousand charging buffalo.

They all jumped and jerked back as the thundering sound of splintering wood crashed down all around them. The roof was literally lifted from its four walls and heaved up and away. The door came next, lifted from its hinges and flung back so that now a bare open space stood before them. All eyes were nailed to that wide-open space, peering out into a black night and then he was there, standing in the doorway, his eyes moving over their cages until they rested on the one cage he sought.

A soldier walked up next to him.

"All right Officer Ballisto," he half turned, never taking his eyes off the one female he came to take out of here and never let go of. His breath left his body as his eyes bore into hers. She stood at the cage door with her fore arm wrapped around her niece. He would spend a lifetime making sure that she never saw the inside of another cage again.

Senior Officer Ballisto turned and said to a crowd of soldiers now gathered behind them. "Release them and take them to the perimeters, then start on the second shed. Make sure that not one wall is left standing. General's orders."

Zeto scurried up onto the shelves where all the cages sat, followed by several soldiers who were beginning to rip down the walls. He couldn't hear the yelling, and cheering his former cellmates were making as the soldiers began working to release their locks... or the walls crashing out in one solid heap onto the frosty ground... he held only *her* in his line of vision....

"*You da minkman! Da MINKMAN!!!*" screamed Venanzio as Zeto passed his cage. They were all banging on the walls of their wire mesh cages screaming his name. He stood in front of Adrianna's removing his eyes from hers only to pull the hinge pin from the catch-lock, and pull the latch away. He stood to the left of the cage as the door sprang open and he reached inside and grabbed her out and into his arms.

Adrianna reached around his neck with her forearms and

held him tightly. She could feel his heart racing next to hers. He stepped back and looked into her face. He reached up and touched her cheeks and smoothed the fur on the sides of her face. He kissed her nose and her head and her eyes and her mouth and then he reached down and grabbed little Marcellina into his arms and spun her around and said, "My girls! Can you walk?"

Adrianna swung her hind legs back and forth. Both were stiff and weak from non-use. "They are a bit stiff, but I think if you give me a minute I can manage."

Marcellina jumped up and down as though she were springing on a trampoline. No problems there.

Zeto looked down at Marcellina. "Grab my tail," he said as he reached out and swung Adrianna up into his arms and began to carry her past the now empty cages along the outer shelving.

"Zeto!," Adrianna squealed. "I can walk. You can't carry me down... there," she pointed toward the ground.

"Marcellina, clutch onto the fur on my back." Before Adrianna could squirm out of his arms, all three landed on the floor of a now demolished shed. Zeto stood tall as he carried both of his girls from the place that would not longer exist after tonight. He listened to the crashing of roofs and walls as they fell to the ground along with the shelves and cages that were being toppled and destroyed… smiling all the way.

He strode with his soon to be bride, to the perimeter where the General stood watching it all. She would live her days as she wanted as long as she agreed to be his.

"Count Ulderico!" he heard someone yell from behind. He turned and saw Beppe smiling with a female mink that was also in her twilight years. The two held fast, clasping each other around the waist. "My wife Count. My wife."

Zeto could feel himself well up. What was happening to him? Was he turning into some kind of emotional Pollyanna jellyfish?

"Nice to meet you Signora Beppe," he said as he continued walking.

It was easy for him to locate the Grand General who, at the moment, was surrounded by a small group of minks that had been released from the first two sheds that now lay in rumbles.

The Polecats were working on the third and fourth sheds simultaneously while mink and badger soldiers headed for the north face to release the thousands of minks, genetically considered wild, into their freedom.

The General scrutinized Zeto as he approached with a beautiful female mink in his arms and a young female minky hanging around his neck. Now wasn't that a picture. He smiled at the sight.

"I think you can put me down now," Adrianna whispered into Zeto's ear just before they reached the General.

Little Marcellina jumped off Zeto's back and walked around to stand in front of her aunt.

Zeto released Adrianna as Marcellina reached up to hold his free paw. "Adrianna, this is the Grand General of His Majesty

Royal Military, Minister of Defense, General Tito DiNicolantonio who made all of this possible. General this is Adrianna Benini and her niece Marcellina Benini."

Adrianna walked up to the Grand General and extended her paw and shook his outstretched one. "General, I can never thank you enough for what you are doing here tonight. Tonight is historical. It will be written in every history book across the nation what you have accomplished here. I can only imagine the bravery and courage it took to lead these soldiers tonight into this human realm, one that has never been punctured before."

She reached down and picked up his paw, speckled with gray, and kissed the very top. "You have given all of us our lives back; my niece now has a future because finally our species has sent a very serious message after tonight that we will tolerate no more."

He smiled down at her and thought that Zeto had made a good match. Yes… definitely a wise choice. "This will make the next farm and the farm after that much harder a conquest. But I cannot take credit for this Signorina Adrianna. My soldiers make me look good."

He turned to Zeto. "And you Count, should be commended for all the courageous feats you have hurtled in the past ten days."

Everyone surrounding the general cheered and grabbed at Zeto, some patting his back, other hugging him, when suddenly a thought popped into his brain.

"Where's Mooch?" He looked up at the sudden stillness that fell over the group. He watched each one of them lower their heads. "Where is he?" No one would look up or make eye contact with him.

"I had completely forgotten about him with everything that is going on. What is the matter with all of you? Why aren't any of you looking at me?"

Adrianna stepped forward and placed her paws on his cheeks. "Tucci took him Zeto. We haven't seen or scented him from the morning after you left."

"What do you mean Tucci took him? Where did he take him?" He looked at Adrianna, feeling a sickening drop in his stomach. "Where?"

"None of us know. Tucci was livid thinking that Mooch had eaten his best pelt. He bought our plan, rock, stock and barrel. He then proceeded to man-handle Mooch's cage, saying that he wouldn't give him one more thing to eat until he was ready to-to, *you know*."

Zeto raked his claws through the fur on the top of his head. His heart flurried and his breath started to speed.

"Well... I have got to find him. Did he say anything else that you can remember?"

"He did... Mooch said it, I remember," Edna interjected." He said something that none of us truly understood. He told us to tell you that he *"didn't release."*

"Oh jeez....Oh boy..." Zeto squeezed the top of his head with both paws. "I have got to go find him! I just hope I am not too late...." He looked over at the General.

"Keep these two with you. Please. Don't lose sight of them. I've got to go back and find Mooch. I will be able to detect his scent quicker than any of your soldiers."

"Listen Zeto... before you go," the General said with eyes that suddenly looked grave. "Prepare yourself. He may be one of the ones that we didn't get to in time. Our satellite pictures show a repository on the west perimeter, a refrigerated storehouse containing pelts. If you cannot find him, you may want to search in there. Take Colonel Lugasteino with you. Go search for him, but prepare yourself."

Zeto turned in haste, refusing to believe for a minute that what was left of Mooch laid on a table or hung in a refrigerated storehouse. He ran toward what was left of the eight bunkers to search there first. *Mooch was not in that repository* he refused to believe it....

Colonel Lugasteino and a few COBRA soldiers followed behind Zeto as he took off in the direction of the eighth shed. He would go to the back barracks in hopes of finding Mooch in one of the cages there if he wasn't among the minks freed in the eighth shed....

The Colonel and his men reached the eighth shed before the Polecats got there. They were now working on shed six and seven. In a matter of minutes, the locks on the shed door were picked and they all entered a darkened cubbyhole. An unclean blackness permeated; cages lined both sides of the shed, up and down, but an eerie dolefulness prevailed. The cages were full of minks, two, some three to a cage, but they said nothing as Zeto and the rest of the soldier minks filed in. Zeto could not scent Mooch. He knew as soon as he walked in that shed that he had never been taken there.

He looked over and back at the rows of minks stuffed in cages sizes smaller than the cages he and his cellmates had been in. They sat perfectly still. Zeto breathed deep. What was wrong with them? Why did they just sit there motionless and stare and say nothing?

Colonel Lugasteino and his men began to remove locks and open cages and still they sat, saying nothing, not moving just sitting and staring like zombies.

"Fellow minks you are free." Zeto pronounced with impatience creeping in his voice.

Zeto could see slight movement in a few of the cages as many of them stirred. A few of the minks began to rise and try to walk outside on the ledge as though they were in a dream. What was wrong with them, he wondered? *Had they been drugged?*

"This is no vision," a rather thin mink said to his bunkmate. His fur was thick and shined like glass. Shocked, he added, "I think this is the real-deal. The noise we have been hearing, the cheering and hollering, I believe this is all real Fobio."

A mink with a gleaming flaxen pelt, one called Fobio, stood and exited his cage as the rest of them followed. He shook is long blondish mane. "It is real." He winced as he tried stretching his hind legs. He stood moving stiff limbs back and forth trying to feed moving blood into his stiffened joints, his hind paws buckled as he tried to get them to move. Many were going to need help because their legs could no longer carry them out.

"This is real," Zeto said, noticing they were all moving at a snails pace; some could not move at all, but then he realized that these minks had been caged for near to eight months. No wonder they moved slowly. It was a miracle a few could move at all. "These soldiers will help you down and will take you to medics."

"You mean that we are saved? That tomorrow morning we will be home with our families and not...."

"Yes. You are free and can go back to your families. If you need medical assistance, there are Wolverine medics on property perimeters. They will assist you. Colonel Lugesteino, get them out of here. They need help moving. I am going to the north face with the rest of the badgers and royal mink militia. I will search there."

Zeto turned and ran in the direction where the back barracks stood. To him, it looked like tidal waves of minks being scattered and freed, scampering and heading for the woodlands. As hard as he tried, he could not pick up any trace scents of Mooch. He ran throughout two massive structures housing up to twenty-five thousand minks, and went back again searching and hunting--trying to pick up something and still there was no scent of him. It was as though he had just vanished.

Several COBRA soldiers accompanied him and they also

continued to scent, but again, came up empty. Zeto pressed his paws over the sides of his temples, applying pressure and closed his eyes. A profound sickness twisted at his insides. He knew where he had to go next. Dread darkened the recesses of thought. He walked slowly with soldiers following behind.

...The Repository stood alone. Of course, he knew that it would be standing off by itself, tucked ever so cozily beneath large evergreens, and Blue Spruces. Zeto held his breath, but he harbored hope that Mooch would not be among the lost, the ones that could not be saved. His heart hammered and a tiny pulse beat against his temples. He turned around to face the few COBRA soldiers that stood behind him and motioned for them to blast down the door.

A few minutes later they stood at the open entrance staring into freezing darkness. Zeto did not know if he had the stomach to cross its threshold.

"Someone... find the lights," he said softly.

He stood and waited while the soldiers moved into the room. He shuddered as he walked into the lighted room and stood in shocked silence...

From a high flat ceiling hung mounds of mink pelts in a great array of colors and sizes, tables strewn about held more pelts some spread flat and appeared, to him to be drying. *Blood and skin drying.* The mere sight of it sickening him.

"W-w-what kind of person could do this? I cannot. I just cannot."

233

Zeto turned, with his back facing a few COBRA soldiers that began scenting and when he was finished, he turned and fled from the room.

Zeto was sweating heavily and his stomach churned as he scrambled outside. Bile rose in his throat. Numbed by what he had just seen, shocked beyond words, Zeto rested his forehead against the trunk of a large tree, until the dizziness passed. COBRA soldiers were busy disassembling the repository as he stood valiantly trying not to lose all the contents in his stomach. How could he scent Mooch in a place so saturated with the scent of slaughter? Weak, and sick at heart, he stood straight and walked slowly, pausing periodically to sniff the crisp night air. *Still there was nothing.*

How could this be? What had Tucci done with him? Did he sale and ship him like a parcel package? This night, starry skied and clear would not give him one small trace scent of Mooch.... Again, his stomach fluttered. He *knew* the odds of finding Mooch alive was diminishing. He swore to himself that he would get answers if he had to beat it out of Tucci before the night's end.

"Who's there...?" Zeto jumped, suddenly turning to look toward the weathered wood of Tucci's dilapidated garage. He stopped and listened. Did he hear something inside? He stood perfectly still, not moving a muscle, just staring toward the old garage that no one had given a second glance to this entire night....

He heard buzzing in his ear... and muffled sounds of something inside. *Movement.* Zeto started quickly toward the garage door and listened.

More movement....

Hurriedly he fumbled with the door and squeezed inside. He opened wood paneled garage doors wider allowing more light in and carefully surveyed it. Tucci's old tan pick-up truck sat in the shadows with its headlights facing the doors. He had backed the truck in; the flatbed was almost touching the back wall with several tarpaulins thrown over it. Zeto stood in the doorway of the darkened garage, listening. He started toward a movement he heard underneath the tarp and started to grab at the edges hanging over the side. He was picking up a scent, but it was weak. When minks began to die, their scents died with them.

"Is that you Zeto? It smells like you...."

"*Mooch! Mooch!*" He pulled furiously at a heavy layer of tarp covering the flat bed.

"*Zeto!*" Mooch sounded out of breath...." I knew you could do it... you gotta get me outta here cousin! I can hardly breathe. That nasty old coot is trying to starve and suffocate me to death. He wants me to die slowly. *You gotta get me outta here. I can hardly breathe.*"

"I am going as fast as I can...." Zeto continued to tug at the heavy canvas material. "Try to stay calm Mooch. Conserve your air. I may need to go get help. This may be too heavy for me to lift alone."

"*Noooooooooo.... please don't leave me... please....*" Mooch begged. "*You can do it!*"

"Okay.... Calm down Mooch.... I'm not going anywhere

until I can get you out of here. But you need to quit talking. Your air supply is what is important right now and I don't want you to waste it by talking. Try to relax and I will get you out. "

Zeto's claws never stopped pulling. "From what I understand, you haven't had any food for three days. That had to have been tough for you. Just think when I get you out of here, we can go back to Crabby's and you can eat all the crab cakes your heart desires. No Road Kill, unless I can take the COBRA unit with me... Mooch! Are you listening?"

"Yeah," Mooch whispered weakly.

"Okay... just wanted to make sure. The COBRA, I'm sure you have never heard of them... even _I_ had never heard of them. They are Prince Montego's big secret. They are an elite group of specialists equivalent to the human Navy Seals that we use to read about.

Remember how we loved to read about the exploits of those invincible Navy Seals? Well, this group could give them a run for their money. When I get you out of here you are not going to believe the mink-power right outside. They have freed the entire farm Mooch...."

With his claws buried deep into the fabric, Zeto pulled with all his strength until the first tarp finally fell to the floor.

"Listen to me Mooch. I am going to climb up there and puncture holes in the next couple layers of tarp so that we won't have to worry so much about the amount of air getting in. Maybe I can rip a hole big enough to get in and get you out of there that way.

Just try to relax. Alright?"

"Alright. I'm okay cousin... now that you're here."

"Okay, my friend. Just be patient."

Zeto hauled himself up on the truck's flatbed with a grunt and immediately went to work on the thick canvas with his claws. This tarp was older, more brittle, dry rotted and in no time, Zeto had punctured a large hole in it. He ripped and tore a slash long enough so that he could now see and feel the outline of Mooch's cage.

"Tell me more of what's been going on out there?" Mooch whispered, sounding more exhausted by the minute.

"Make sure you are lying on the bottom, Mooch. I am coming though the top of your cage now and one slip and my claws will go right through even your hard head." Zeto chuckled as he held the tarp tightly with one paw while the other paw, swung down through the material, cutting through, shredding it into ribbons and exposing the top of the metal cage that Mooch was laying in the bottom of.

"Hey Mooch...." Zeto stood on the top of the crate looking down at his best friend curled in a fetal position on the floor of his cage. Mooch looked up at him and smiled.

"Do you think you can walk Mooch?" Zeto asked working his way down the front to the cage door.

"I think. I'm a little wobbly, but I know I am going to need some extensive psychotherapy after this."

Mooch stood up. "Ahhhhhhhhhh.... This air feels

wonderful." He inhaled deeply and started to stand while Zeto continued to rip more of the canvas into bigger holes as he dropped down and stood in front of the wire mesh cage door. He fumbled with the metal pin until he finally forced it up and out of its slot and opened the door.

Mooch moved unsteadily toward him; telltale signs of his ordeal appeared in dirty debris matted fur plastered down with large chunks of it missing altogether, and Zeto noticed that he was significantly thinner yet his enclosure was still a tight fit. A box that allowed no room for movement.

Zeto held his arm out for his cousin to take. "Grab a hold of my arm Mooch."

Mooch held onto Zeto's arm and waddled out of his prison door, bowing his head as if in silent prayer. "I never thought I would see you again my friend. I thought I would either starve to death or die from lack of oxygen."

"A lot of faith you had in me..." Zeto chuckled.

"No I had faith in you, really I did Zeto... but after all these weeks, I guess I just finally grew tired. I didn't think I would be around to see you liberate this place."

"Lack of food... being cramped in a cage so small you can't even stretch... covered with canvas so you can't breath properly... that would just about do anyone in, but here you are. Come on Mooch...lean on me... let's get out of here...."

Mooch and Zeto talked quietly as they made their way down from the flat bed and onto the garage floor. Mooch recovered with each step of his new found freedom, feeling air fill his lungs and the promise of another day beating in his heart. He let go of Zeto's arm once they reached the open garage doors and turned.

"What went on here tonight? I heard screaming and running about and buildings sounding like they were being torn apart... but was too weak to even cry out. What has happened?"

"What has happened here will go down in our history... something that has never happened before. Every mink that was alive here tonight has been freed."

"How did this happen? And Tucci. Where is Tucci?"

"Let's just say that Tucci and his wife are being detained and restrained, in what I would call a hog-tied fashion."

Mooch's eyes widened. "You mean he knows? That he is actually aware, that he has seen our species in action?"

Zeto's lips quirked upward. "Ohhhhhh indeed he has. I would say that he has definitely seen our soldiers in action, as well as the badger soldiers, and we can't forget the polecats or the wolverines."

Mooch stared at Zeto for several seconds. "Please don't tease me Zeto... please. I am too weak at the moment and my heart can't take a practical joke. Tell me you're serious."

Zeto smiled vaguely. "Mooch, look at me. You probably know me better than most anyone. How many practical jokes have you ever seen me play?"

"None." Mooch grinned. "Never in fact. Can you imagine? I can't believe this. Please Zeto. You must grant me one wish of an almost dead mink...."

"You're looking more alive to me by the moment, maybe a bit worse for wear but alive and on the mend. But go ahead. What is it that you want?"

Mooch looked past Zeto over to a very large cage that sat in the corner of the garage. It was a cage that probably housed twenty or more minks at one time. "See that cage over there?"

Zeto turned and looked. "Yes. What about it?"

"I saw that cage almost four days ago when Tucci brought me in here and the only thing I could think about... dream about, nay, even wish for, is that someday I would be able to stuff his big fat never-ending rear-end into one of his own cages and let him experience first hand what it feels like to be trapped like the rat that he is.

Let's see how much he fancies not being able to move about or to be able to feed himself when hungry, --let him know what it feels like to sit in freezing temperatures on frozen ground feeling as the clock slowly ticks all warmth leave your limbs except for the painful pin pricks of blood that has failed to move and has finally stopped, the complete loss of time to the point of not being able to process logically ... let him feel the smattering of being *locked in.*

He moved in the direction of the cage. "This one there would be tight, but with a little finagling and the help of a few of those COBRA's you spoke of, I am sure we could ram him into one. Oh please... you have got to let me do this...."

Zeto's eyes twinkled merrily and a slow crooked smile softened his face. "In all honesty Mooch, when I saw that cage, that was the first thing that went through my mind also. But don't you think that would put us on his same level?"

"Yes. It would, and it will feel *so* great."

Zeto, patted Mooch's back, as they headed for the garage opening. "Let me run it by the Grand General."

"He's here?" Mooch was almost speechless.

"Headed the entire operation into the human realm. He is here. Let's go talk to him. I am sure he wouldn't mind our little venture. He seems like a mink with a sense of humor...."

Signore Tucci's big red enraged face stared out at the gathered crowd of soldiers and freed minks that surrounded him as he looked out at them from behind a locked wire mesh door. He had struggled, had wiggled and jerked about gallantly, but Zeto, Mooch and a several COBRA soldiers were stronger. Together they stuffed Tucci into a cage where all movement was inhibited and slammed the door and locked it. Tucci's eyes widened as he listened, understanding every word they spoke.

Mooch stepped forward, while everyone cheered and applauded, especially Edna and Samone. The sky grew paler and he suddenly realized that he could hear birds chirping from someplace close by.

So the day has broken.

He walked over to face Signore Tucci, and the crowd grew

quiet. *"Friends...Romans...Countryminks, lend me your ear..."* Mooch looked up toward the lightening sky and loud enough for the entire crowd to hear, he said, *"Hey...little buddy...Rise and Shine Mr. Sleepy Head...* I'm talking to you Tucci. Are you ready for this!"

No one flinched.

Slowly Mooch turned around, bent over slightly so that his back-bottom was pressed flesh against Tucci's cage door, and without a beat, lifted his long tail up... up... up to release almost two weeks worth of terror and he made sure he put it right there right smack against his face.

"Grrrrr....." he pushed.... "Grrrrrrrrrrrrrr." He pushed some more until finally he had worked up a power ball so potentially revolting that even he would have to move quickly to get out of the way.

"Grraaaaaaaaaaaaahhhhhhhh...." He let it rip.... He turned around and faced Tucci again; he knew, for the very last time, and through a thick cloud of vaporous gas permeated, one that gagged him, he managed to say, *"Gotta get that fresh morning air. Make it a good one!"*

Mooch turn and fled with a laughing crowd that had already started toward the forest, never turning back.

* * * *

Chapter 11

The Wedding Feast

Villa de Castello was alight with lamps, candelabra, and chandeliers; music drifted through closed windows as a full minstrel played classically impassioned love songs. A silent wintry mist lingered over fresh snow-enshrouded hills, while inside crystal champagne glasses clinked together in celebratory jubilation. There was much rejoicing this night and there was no place grander than Castello Di Ulderico to do it. Castello di Ulderico's formal ballroom was opened to honor the newly wedded Count Zeto Pateleone Ulderico and his bride of three hours.

The Count looked around at all the merrymaking and found himself wondering if providence had lead him to this moment? Standing alone, in this familiar corner, where he had stood many times before seemed like a lifetime ago. Today he had watched and listened to every mink that had ever meant anything to him, raise their glass and drink a toast to his health, his happiness and his luck in finding her. His eyes moved over to his bride as she tilted her head to listen to something apparently amusing that his Uncle Angelo had just whispered into her ear because she looked back up at him and began to laugh. What a picture. Uncle Angelo and his Adrianna laughing.

He loved to watch her laugh. Nothing in this world was more satisfying. She dazzled him; she dazzled everyone. And tonight, --well--tonight she looked more like a Queen than a mere Contessa, more beautiful and regal than he thought possible in her wedding gown, the same gown his mother had worn so many years ago when she had married his father, and with a few alterations here and there, the soft silk pearl encrusted gown looked as though it had been made especially for her.

The only shadow of sadness that had fallen upon this special day had been that her father, a father that she had once adored, was not there to walk her down the aisle.

He looked over at the Grand General swirling his mother around on the dance floor. They waltzed as though they were both eighteen again, and Zeto had to admit that he revered this mink more than anyone else he had ever known for so many reasons and in so many ways.

The General had actually shown him what it was like to stand up and be a mink. That it was of no consequence the status one possessed, but what one did for their fellow mink with that status that counted. A life was a life, and every living soul was somebody to someone. He had shown him how substance and strength were measured. Such a powerhouse in position and reputation and still he remained a humble servant to all of Italy and beyond its borders.

It amazed him that this mink, that held such a lofty position, had decided to stay two days hence and had volunteered his arm to Adrianna, who warmly accepted it. She told him that he honored her by walking her down the aisle to her groom. And so it had been. …His Adrianna holding on to the Minister of Defense as he walked her down the aisle and gave her away.

Zeto held his champagne glass up to his lips and took another sip. The chilled liquid bubbled down his throat. He grinned as he looked about the room. Life looked so different from where he was standing. He never imagined that he could be this happy.

Prince Montega stood in the center of a small group of dignitaries, sipping wine and leaning his head to the right to listen to something Alfonso Bappia, his Minister of Agriculture was saying.

The Prince, black pelt, gray eyed, was the most elegant of the group, yet there was an underlying current of alertness under his velvety veneer--nothing got passed him. He was an agile ruler, had hand selected each of his ministers and worked from a position as being a team player. No decision was made for the good of the minks in Italy without all of his Ministers present and heard.

Zeto admired him for being the first ruler in a long string of many; to intercede, to take that first step, which was always the hardest, and to get involved, to finally say, *"No more."* He was now a more popular and celebrated prince than ever before.

At first Zeto thought it was unfortunate that the humans believed that Signore Tucci and his wife had calculated and executed the destruction of their own farm for insurance purposes. No one believed their outlandish claims that an army of animals had destroyed their farm and released all the minks into the wilderness. They said it had been an *"inside job."*

247

So with justice being served the humans locked both of them behind bars for a long time for attempted insurance fraud. It had been all over the newspapers, and the Grand General gleefully rejoiced that the human's premise could work to their advantage for future invasions. Zeto saw the logic in it.

Savoring the champagne as he took another sip, he held it in his mouth for a few seconds, as his eyes moved to his mama ~forever youthful. She was being gracefully whisked around the ballroom floor, gazing up at the mink she had loved so many years before. Funny that she had never mentioned the General in all these years. Right now she exuded happiness dancing with his paw tightly encircling her waist as they moved with each step to the music. He noticed that she had shed her perpetual black *mourning* dress in favor of a crisp indigo blue gown.

Surely a month ago, witnessing this, would have incensed him as showing some kind of disrespect to the memory of his father, but Zeto had changed, his experience taught him a lesson in temperance and acceptance. If this is what made his mother happy, so be it. She would not hear any protest form him.

He leaned back against the wall and shot a quick glance over at Mooch, who never left the hors d' oeuvre table for long. He was maybe a tad thinner than Zeto could ever remember, and Mooch preened like a peacock at his new slimmer look. After having been cleaned and groomed, his pelt was now on the mend; it appeared fuller and healthier than it had in years. Edna stood next to him, fed him a morsel of something scrumptious the cook had prepared all while little Samona held tightly onto his hand.

He shook his head and smiled over at the picture they made... they had all been forever altered. He could not imagine going back to the life he had. He looked around the room and one by one he spotted each and every bunkmate that had shared Shed #1 with him.

Beppe came with the wife he had been willing to die with, sitting on a settee after all those years of marriage, still holding hands and engrossed in conversation. Venanzio brought his *"hot babe"* and was now circling the room, waiting for music, as he said, "he could like...dance to." They all brought that special someone and that special magic with them. Then he looked back at her.

He pushed himself off the wall with his hind leg and deposited his champagne glass on a side table as he walked onto the dance floor toward her. He tapped his Uncle Angelo on the back.

"May I dance with my wife?" He said looking over his Uncle Angelo's shoulder at her.

"Ohhhhhh... of course son... I'm sorry. I seem to have been monopolizing your bride," Uncle Angelo said, moving aside.

Zeto took Adrianna into his arms and refocused on her face, into light amber eyes, thick black lashes, pert snout and lips that smiled up at him. His eyes misted as her gaze fixed. Someone once told him that males fell in love with their eyes and that females fell in love with their ears. He had been lucky... he had fallen in love with both.

"Contessa Adrianna Ulderico," he began, a lazy, crooked smile that triggered her heart to move a little faster. "That does have a nice ring."

"And would equally be so as a mere Signora," she twirled one of his whiskers."

"I don't believe I have thanked you properly…."

A puzzled look flashed over the new Contessa's face, but her smile never wavered. She could feel his paw around her waist tightening as they glided along the dance floor.

"Thank me for what my Count?" Her gloved paw moved back to his shoulder.

"For saying "*yes*'" when I asked you... for accepting my paw in marriage…."

"Oh... that?" She leaned in closer tipping her head upward as he bent his head down so that he could hear her over the music. In his ear, Contessa Adrianna of Ulderico whispered softly. "My dearest Count... such an ordeal that started all this; an ordeal that I would do all over again if it meant that you would forever give me a lifetime of this…."

"A lifetime of dancing and merrymaking?"

"No, my Lord," she murmured against his ear. "A lifetime of love."

He stopped and cupped his paws on either side of her face. "A lifetime of love?" He asked as he gently kissed the tip of her nose. "You have that Contessa. You will always have it... a lifetime of love it is."

...Count Zeto Pantaleone Ulderico came from a long line of Roman counts and contessas. In another lifetime, you could often find him at Castello di Ulderico, his palace den, surrounded by an army of guards, servants and a handful of friends, showing off portraits of family members that had in one way or another become ornaments around famous humans' necks....

Now you could find Zeto surrounded by an army of friends and family sharing a repast, outside playing lawn games, inside playing board games, or out dancing and dining with his new wife.

Zeto no longer turned the pages of a very large family album he used to display on his coffee table, a book he once considered his favorite. He wondered spiritedly what he had ever found interesting about articles of clothing exhibiting a century of dead relatives? That book had been whisked to the attic to collect dust with the rest of the items of bygone days. Sometimes it was hard to believe how stuck in the past he used to be.

Another book, his favorite, occupied his coffee table. This book was filled with wedding pictures and birthday celebrations and friends out playing and laughing and eating fried earthworms with secret sauce.

For Zeto, life was good. Living life and making good memories...that's what counted. He would always remember that day when all choices were taken away, that day when his life was no longer his own. He was forgetting nothing and as long as he wasn't forgetting he would always remember. Yes. Life was good.

Robyn Rolison-Hanna is a teacher of children with special needs as well as secondary education. She lives in Pennsylvania with her husband and Goldendoodle, Tallulah. This is her first novel.

www.zetothemink.com

Cover Artwork and Interior Illustrations
By Olga Dunayeva

www.dunayeva.com

Printed in the United States
204009BV00002B/112-210/P

9 780981 747231